Dresses and other CATASTROPHES

Dani O'Connor

Spinsters Ink
2008

Spinsters Ink
P.O. Box 242
Midway, Florida 32343

Printed in the United States of America on acid-free paper
First Edition

Editor: Katherine V. Forrest
Cover designer: Linda Callaghan

ISBN: 1-883523-97-4
ISBN: 978-1-883523-97-8

To Erik—my favorite travel companion and unconditional friend.

Bio

Dani O'Connor remains optimistic.

Chapter 1

It came as no surprise to anyone that our plans for marriage were delayed, and sidelined, and delayed again.

That was what was to be expected from two individuals like us—procrastinators. It wasn't that we were too busy, or too work driven or even too scared; we were just distracted by shiny objects.

A few years ago while at a furniture store near our home in Dallas, I asked Sam to marry me. We were arguing over styles of sofas, and I fell in love with one. She told me if I loved the sofa so much, I should marry it. I decided to offer to marry her instead.

Immediately after our retail engagement we had to deal with family events—the marriage of Sam's brother, Toby, to a singing superstar named Amelia, and the enormous undertaking of my coming out to my parents. Anyone who has ever come out to her parents knows that it takes some time for everyone to adapt. I put off the marriage plans for a bit in hopes my parents would embrace my lifestyle and partner and be willing to attend our wedding ceremony. Sam was busy dealing with her family's hotel business and problems while juggling her law practice. She wanted her family to be somewhat functional before we headed off to wed so none of their drama would be a distraction.

Those were our excuses. We claimed we were simply waiting to get all our family ducks in a row so we could focus on our monumental milestone. I guess if I were to analyze it now, I would realize we were just making excuses for fear of the unknown.

We had been engaged for two years and still had not purchased rings. All we had was the monstrosity of a red leather sofa to symbolize our spur-of-the-moment engagement. We talked about jewelry a lot—our style preferences, cost, color and even measured our fingers. Her finger was half a size larger than mine, which meant she was entitled to more diamonds, according to her. My thought was that since she had larger hands, she wore the pants in the family and was not entitled to any jewels whatsoever. We opted to arm wrestle to see who got to choose the rings. She won, probably because she had larger hands. I reluctantly left the jewelry decisions up to her.

My job was to pick a location for the wedding. Neither of us committed to settling on a specific wedding day. We always said this fall or next summer, which usually turned into next fall or early spring. Choosing the locale for the ceremony was simple enough. We initially intended on marrying in Amsterdam, and neither of us gave it a second thought, so my job was done. The wedding would take place in Amsterdam on a day to be determined and with jewelry still pending.

Unlike most couples who talked about wedding plans incessantly with friends and family, we mentioned it maybe once a week at most, and usually very casually or in jest. We made remarks like, "You know you won't get away with that shirt once we're married." Or, "No wife of mine will take tequila shooters from a cross-dressing monkey." We were so flippant about the wife situation that it seemed as though neither of us took it seriously. Admittedly, it was difficult to get too sincere about a ceremony or commitment that wouldn't be legally recognized in our home state of Texas. The ceremony itself was merely a gesture to show our love and loyalty toward one another. Still we both conceded it was an important and necessary phase in our relationship—practically an obligation. That's how it works; you meet, fall in love, move in together, get married, have kids and live happily ever after. There's a slight difference for gay people; you meet (in a gay bar or on the Internet), fall in love (within ten days of meeting), move in together (within three months of meeting), get married (not really, but you can pretend), have kids or 'gaybies' (via pricey adoptions or sterilized turkey basters) and live happily ever after (despite awkward family events and legal technicalities). So maybe we were a bit dismissive about the scenario, but I knew deep down inside that I did want to spend my life with Sam, and I felt the feeling was mutual. I decided once and for all that after years of procrastinating, it was time to start moving forward with our plans. We needed to get married so we could begin the "happily ever after." I took it upon myself to start the planning process by being as subtle as possible.

Chapter 2

It was the night before my thirty-sixth birthday and Sam and I lay in bed watching Cartoon Network's Adult Swim. "So, Doctor O'Connor. What do you want for your birthday?"

I hated it when she called me Doctor. It was like she was making a dig about the fact that I wasn't currently utilizing my education in a career. I preferred to simply be called, Doc. At least then I could assume she was referring to my initials and not my shortcomings. "My birthday's tomorrow, Sammy. Are you gonna run out to Wal-Mart tonight and get me something? Shouldn't you have asked this question...I don't know...three hours ago, before the mall closed?" I knew she had already bought me something because a box had arrived in the mail days earlier.

"Yeah, well Wal-Mart has some good specials, and it's never crowded this time of night. What do you want?" She rolled onto her side and played with my hair.

I fidgeted with the buttons on her cotton monkey pajamas. "I don't know. I haven't given it much thought." I lied; I had hoped for her to ask the very question.

"Right. You've had a pensive look for a week. I know there's some thought process going on in there."

I tried to avoid the topic as long as possible by looking around the room. I admired the bedroom's stone fireplace and thought about how I needed to clean the cobwebs off the mantel. I debated the wall color and wondered if bright red really was a good idea. Finally, I took a deep breath and spat it out. "I want us to finalize the plans and get married once and for all." I could feel my face flush.

"Wow. I was thinking of something more like an Atari or Cabbage Patch doll." She laughed. I loved the way her dimples fell into place when she smiled. She was getting the characteristic crow's feet that were so prominent in the Laine family. She was aging so gracefully and I couldn't help but feel ancient in comparison.

"How can you possibly be living in the eighties? Were you even born yet when those things existed? The Atari is now the Wii, and the Cabbage Patch is...well, actually it's making a comeback."

"Okay, so you want to get married for your birthday? Like tomorrow?" She raised her voice and I could tell I was already starting to stress her out.

"I don't want to have the ceremony tomorrow, but I do want us to sit down and commit to a date."

"You mean we can bring dates to our wedding? Cool, there's this new girl at the office I could ask. I think she'd be the perfect wedding date. Looks good in heels."

I didn't know whether to laugh or cry. "Funny. If you're gonna be an ass about this, then maybe you should ask her out. I want to commit to doing this, Sam. I want to marry you and I want to know right now if you want to marry me."

She fell silent. By the way she furrowed her brow, it looked like she was trying to think of something to say, but instead she pressed her perfect lips tightly together, and then covered her face with the monkey pillow that matched her pajamas.

"Are you kidding me? You? The fancy lawyer who never shuts her mouth has no rebuttal? No answer? Nothing? It's a simple question and you're silent? What? Thinking? Debating? Finding kind words to let me down easy?" I started to panic.

"Look, birthday girl, why don't we save this discussion for another time? You know I love you, but there's a lot going on with our families, my work, your...well, there's not a good time to plan a trip any time soon."

"First of all, I didn't ask if you loved me. I asked if you still wanted to marry me. Secondly, what's up with the pause?

Just because I'm not teaching right now doesn't mean I'm not working."

"Doc, you wrote a wonderful book. You sold eleven copies worldwide. I'm very proud of you. But ever since the book came out, all you do is stare at a blank canvas or a blank computer screen. You haven't painted anything in months. The only thing I've seen you write is a check to Pizza Hut."

"Was that a remark about my weight? Are you calling me fat and lazy?"

She fought a smile. "No, baby. I'm just saying maybe now isn't the time to discuss marriage. You're not fat. You're not lazy. The kitchen has never been cleaner."

"Yeah. Because I ate all the food." I was definitely on the defensive and she knew it.

"No, because you've done a wonderful job of taking care of the house." She sounded a little condescending.

"Then I'd be the perfect wife—a domestic goddess." I couldn't believe the words were coming from my mouth.

"There's nothing domestic about you, Doc. Please get some sleep. We'll discuss a wedding another time. Tomorrow's a big day." She stroked my hair again and it seemed condescending. "Go to sleep. I love you."

"I love you too. And for the record, I sold eleven hundred copies, not eleven. Ass." I couldn't help but feel that I'd won the battle even though she didn't give me what I wanted.

"That's right, sorry." She patted my hip.

She thought she'd won. When she felt victorious, she fell asleep quickly. I could hear her snoring within minutes. This irritated me so instead of forcing myself to try and sleep, I got up, went to our huge walk-in closet and tied the laces of all her shoes together. Once I completed the prank, I drank the rest of the milk from the refrigerator so she wouldn't have any for breakfast. I felt that was enough revenge for one night, so I joined her back in bed and ignored the fact that I had spilled milk down the front of my jog bra and into my cleavage.

I didn't sleep well and woke up on the wrong side of the bed—literally. It happens once in awhile; if I get too restless in my sleep, I start crowding Sam and she climbs over me to make room. She was lying on my side of the bed pretending to be asleep. I knew she had already been up because I smelled fresh coffee and she was dressed and ready for work.

"I know you're not really asleep. You rarely wear a Prada suit to bed."

"Today's a special day. I wore Prada to bed in honor of it." She flattened down the creases on her skirt.

"Right. What's so special about it? It's Friday, you're going to work, I'm mowing the yard and cleaning the house."

"It's my favorite person's birthday, silly." She smiled but still had her eyes closed.

"Today is Dixie Carter's birthday? That's great, honey. Well worth the Prada." I sat on the edge of the bed and stretched.

"Happy Birthday, Dani." She handed me a pink paper-wrapped box. It was much larger than the one that came in the mail, so I knew it wasn't my only gift.

"Oh, Sam. You remembered," I teased and ripped the paper off. Inside was an Atari gaming system. "My goodness. You didn't get this at Wal-Mart did you? Are we in some sort of time warp? Is it nineteen eighty-three again?"

"Yes. You're thirteen today. I bought it on eBay. I thought you might like a blast from the past. Jack told me how the three of you used to play Pitfall for days at a time when you were kids."

"We did. Sometimes all night long." I stared at the plastic joystick and thought about Wyoming summers when Jack, Amy and I would make popcorn and try to conquer the simplistic game. It made me miss my twin sister who'd passed away years earlier from cancer. I looked forward to my birthday call from Jack. "Thank you, Sam. That really means a lot. We can set it up for the party tonight."

She leaned in for a kiss. "I love you, Dani. You're officially the oldest woman I've ever kissed."

"Thanks. I feel ancient. Go to work." I crawled back into bed and pulled the covers over my head.

"I made you breakfast. It's in the microwave. Andrea is coming to mow the yard today. Maybe you could go have lunch.

Get out of the house for once."

"I gotta clean the house. In case you forgot, forty people are coming here tonight to see the world's oldest unemployed fat lesbian."

"You're not old. You're not fat. You're not unemployed. The house is clean enough. And there's only thirty-eight people coming. Tristan and Richard are still in China."

"Any word on the adoption yet?" I walked toward the kitchen as she followed.

"No. Just another delay and more paperwork. I offered legal services, but there's really nothing I can do for them. Tristan is optimistic, but I think Richard is ready to give up and come home."

"We should send them a care package—maybe some pictures from the party and some Texas gourmet treats."

"Does Texas have gourmet food?" She poured me a cup of coffee.

"Salsa. Beef jerky. Tortillas." I racked my brain.

"Okay, maybe the jerky, but the other two are from Mexico and I wouldn't consider them gourmet. Get your breakfast."

I opened the microwave door and found a warm box of Krispy Kremes. "Speaking of gourmet. Did you buy these yourself this morning? Or did Mr. Kreme himself come make them fresh in our kitchen?"

"I bought them last night. But I heated them up myself this morning. Sorry, Doc, I didn't have a lot of time. Oh, we're out of milk. I gotta run. Happy Birthday, relax and enjoy yourself for once. I'll try to be home by three to help with the party stuff." She blew me a kiss and left before I could respond.

I stood in the kitchen with a donut in one hand and a cup of coffee in the other while pondering my existence. I was officially thirty-six. I had taken a leave from my teaching career to explore my creative side. Actually, I was head of the English department at a Women's college. I spent years working my way up, and walked away on a whim, one that I still couldn't explain. In the last couple of years, I'd written one book and sold seven paintings. My total income from that averaged nine hundred dollars a year. I lived with a vivacious lawyer who was thirty pounds lighter, six years younger and millions of dollars richer than I. She was one of those fortunate sorts who got the looks, the brains and the wealthy family. Her parents actually gave her a hotel as a gift. Even though I was relatively intelligent and cute at times, I could never compete with her wealth. I was a kept woman who cleaned toilets and watched made-for-TV movies all day. I realized it was time to wake up and start making changes. I needed to decide if I wanted to go back to my job at the Women's college or if I wanted to write another novel. The big question was, did I really want to start planning the wedding and marry Sam, or was I just looking for a way to be useful and fill the void inside me?

I did nothing important all day long and prayed for a phone call, and the phone never rang. The minute I had conditioner in my hair and shaving cream on my legs, the phone rang. On a normal day, it was most likely to be a solicitor. Despite the Do Not Call List we subscribed to, the telemarketers still found a loophole. I knew on my birthday, however, it was possible that it was a friend calling, so when I heard the phone from the shower, I scrambled out the glass door and slid to the counter to grab the cordless. The caller ID read Jack O'Connor, DDS. My older brother was calling from his office. "Hello Jackie Blue."

"Happy birthday, Dorky O'Connor." His voice sounded forced.

"Thanks. How's life in the dental world today?"

"Same spit, different day." He always said that, and I always laughed. "Whatcha doing for lunch?"

"Sam left me a box of donuts." I tried to sound pathetic and even threw in a little sniffing noise for effect.

"Well, throw the box of carbs into the trash and meet me at Rocket's at noon." His voice started to sound more casual. "We'll share some cheesy fries and a pitcher."

"No carbs there." I laughed. "Okay. Don't let me drink too much. I have to be somewhat sober to prepare for tonight's shindig."

"Whatever you say. See you then, Doctor O'Connor."

"Okay. Hasta, Doctor O'Connor." I hung up and sat down to cry. I knew what lay ahead for our lunch outing. We would make small talk for an hour and after we finished our pitcher one of us would mention the inevitable sadness we felt about Amy. It was impossible to acknowledge my own birthday without thinking about my twin, who used to share every cake and present with me every year until her death. When I stood in her Houston hospital room years earlier and said good-bye, it didn't ever occur to me how every good day from then on would have an overlying cloud of sadness. Hearing Jack's strained voice told me how hard it still was for him to call me and not get to call Amy. I finally made it back to the shower to rinse off my over-conditioned hair when the phone rang again. "Cheeses crackers!" I shouted and slid across the floor once more. "Hello?"

"What's up, Doc?" Sam was calling from her cell phone.

"Just taking a shower." I tried not to sound annoyed. "I'm meeting Jack at noon for lunch at Rocket's. I wish you could join us."

"Rocket's? You're gonna get your drink on, aren't you?"

"We may split a pitcher. I promise to be home by three to get ready for tonight. Were you calling just to get me out of the shower?" I was still dripping wet.

"No, I wanted to see how you're doing." She sighed.

"I'm fine baby. Why?" I asked because sometimes her sensitivity surprised me. She had been a bit callous since she became the high-powered attorney.

"I know that birthdays are a conundrum for you emotionally. You can't celebrate yours without mourning Amy's." Her words sounded rehearsed and I realized she had said the same thing the previous year.

I didn't let on about her lack of originality. "Thank you for worrying. It's hard, but at least I have Jack close. He makes grieving easier and celebrating more fun." I still felt bad that Sam never got to meet Amy and that fact made it hard for us to grieve together.

"He's a great brother. I always wished my brother would grow up and start being more supportive. Tell Jack hello and thank him for the free X-rays."

"Will do, although they were hardly free. You did get him a golf game with his hero, Ben Crenshaw. Where is brother Toby anyway?"

"Um." She paused to think. "Toby and Amelia are still in Germany kicking off her fall tour. I'm sure they'll call or email. I gotta run. Toodles."

I hated when she said toodles and ran. It meant she was lying about something, because even though she's a Dallasite, she still wasn't a toodles type of girl.

I finally finished my shower and headed out for an afternoon with my favorite O'Connor.

Jack was seated in the smoking section when I arrived. In Dallas, the "smoking section" meant "outdoor patio" or "beer garden". It was an unusually warm January day and I was happy to be outside. He greeted me with a bear hug and handed me a plastic tiara.

"I'm not wearing this, Jack. I appreciate that you think I'm a little princess, but it won't match my cowboy boots." I handed the crown back to him. "You wear it. It will look great with your sandals, Sally."

He placed it on his head and sat down without batting an eye. "I ordered us a pitcher and some cheese fries. I wasn't sure if you wanted something else."

"Are you in a hurry? Your office is closed Friday afternoons, right?" I couldn't help but smile at the sight of my muscular brother in princess attire. The color of the crown did nothing for his faded blue scrubs and unshaven face.

"No. We're open. I thought I'd have a few pitchers of beer before I go drill teeth and fix crowns."

"Well, you are the crown princess," I said as I pulled the tiara from his head and tossed it on the table. "So are you mine for the afternoon?"

"Sure. Unless the waitress likes me, then all bets are off."

"I appreciate your taking me to lunch. I was pretty down today."

He took a deep breath and reached for my hand. "I know what you mean. Your birthdays were such an event growing up. How often do you get two parties and two cakes in one weekend? It was like a weeklong celebration. It's still tough to think of your birthday without thinking of Amy."

"I'm sure it always will be. After she died, I didn't want to celebrate the day. But Sam said it was important to her to celebrate my existence and my life. So I guess I kinda got back into the birthday thing for Sam. Plus the gifts are pretty cool." I forced a smile. "Wow, ten whole minutes before you made me cry. That must be a new record."

"I'm sorry, Dani. But we would be remiss if we didn't acknowledge Amy." He poured us each a glass of Miller Lite. "To Amy and Danielle. Happy birthday to my sisters."

I fought a lump in my throat. "To Amy."

We sat in silence for awhile and picked at the fries. I finally decided to share what I had been, as Sam put it, so pensive about over the last week. "I think I'm ready to get married, Jack."

"Well, Doc." He leaned back in his chair and folded his arms. "I don't think the Constitution allows marriage between a sister and a brother, but I appreciate the proposal."

"You're funny for a jackass." I threw a fry at him. "I guess according to the Constitution I can't marry anybody I love then."

"Neither can Catholic priests. So you're not alone." He laughed. "So you and the lawyer are finally going to tie the proverbial knot? It's about time."

"I hate it when you call her the lawyer. You sound like Dad. I told her last night I was ready and she blew me off."

"Did you ask her to marry you, or did you simply say you thought it was time?" He poured another glass of beer.

"What difference does it make?" I reached for a cigarette, then thought of Amy and broke it in half. I couldn't stand the thought of Jack losing another sister to cancer.

"Well, if you made a romantic gesture and asked again if she would marry you, then I'm sure she would have said yes. If you simply said that it's time to get the damn thing over with, then she probably thought you were doing it out of obligation."

"Oh. I don't know. I guess I should have asked."

"Don't dwell on it, Dani. I'm sure she still wants to marry

you. She's stuck around for like eight years now, I don't think she's going anywhere." He motioned to the waitress for another pitcher. "Is that what's got your mind occupied today? You seem distracted?"

"It's just the turning another year older blues. What have I done with my life? Where am I going? Who am I? The normal questions I ask myself every time I feel useless."

"Oh Lord. The early midlife crisis. Should I be a writer, a teacher, a farmer, or a preacher? Should I have a dog, a cat, a fish or kids? Deep in your heart, what do you want to do? You have a rare opportunity to do anything you want."

"Yeah, thanks to the wealth of Samantha Lynne Laine. I wish I had opportunities based on my own success."

"Then reach that success. Write another novel. Paint more, or open a gallery. You were a good teacher, go back to it if you miss it."

"I'm not sure I miss it. I miss having somewhere to be—a reason to get up in the morning."

"I'd think waking up next to a beautiful lady like Sam would be reason enough to get up in the morning." He laughed.

"It is, but she's so busy all the time, it's like she has her own life that often doesn't include me."

"Sam's an extremely driven woman. Her parents put a lot of pressure on her. I keep waiting for the day she finally snaps and moves to Zimbabwe," Jack said.

"Part of me wishes that day would come soon so we could run off and be dreamers together." I sighed.

"You know what you need, Doc? You need a change, something new and impulsive to remind you that you aren't dead yet." He cringed at the statement, probably thinking of Amy.

"And what might that be, Jack? A new midlife crisis sports car, like yours?"

"You need another beer and a trip to the tattoo parlor." The grin on Jack's face was priceless.

"You gotta be kidding me. I can't go get a tattoo today."

"Sure you can. Where do you have to be?"

"I have to meet my girl at the house. We have to get ready

for the party." I was looking for any excuse to avoid admitting that I was a fuddy-duddy.

"Your girl called me this morning and told me to keep you for the day. She has plenty of paid people to get the party preparations taken care of. I'm your escort until five o'clock." He looked at his watch. "That gives us three hours to get lewd, screwed and tattooed."

"Okay, I'm in for the lewd and tattooed part, but you'll have to get screwed on your own."

We made our way to Deep Ellum, a hip part of Dallas populated by nightclubs, eclectic restaurants and tattoo parlors. Jack was a man on a mission, walking into parlor after parlor looking through all the catalogs for the perfect symbolic tattoo. On our fourth stop, he stumbled across a roundish drawing with a star in the middle and fifteen curved points around the perimeter. "This is it, this is the one, I can feel it." He held up the book of sketches from across the room.

I squinted to see the design. "It's really cool-looking, but what does it mean? For all we know, it's the symbol for homophobia."

"Hey, mister." Jack got the tattoo artist's attention. "Is this the symbol for homophobia?"

The guy looked up from his paper. "Nah. That's the symbol for transition. Changing your life. If you want homophobia, you'll have to try a different place. We don't sell hate here, man."

Jack and I laughed. "I think we found the right symbol, and the right shop as well." Jack handed the design book to the guy. "For the lady, make it nice, she's forty today."

"Thirty-six, and please make it as small as possible."

"Can't make it too small lady, the points will blur together. Where do you want it?" He took the book to the copy machine.

"Um, do you have any private rooms?" I blushed.

"Where on your body would you like me to put the tattoo?" He pushed a dreadlock out of his face and batted his long eyelashes.

"Oh. My back, but not in the tramp stamp area. Higher, I

guess, above the bra, below the neck."

"One life transition on the upper back. That's gonna be a hundred bucks. Are you paying, or is it on the homophobe?"

"He's paying for it." I turned to Jack. "Thanks for the tattoo you big homophobe."

"Anytime, you big life-changing homo." He sat down on the worn vinyl sofa and opened his cell phone. "I got calls to make, go with the strange man and let him mar you for life." He snapped his fingers and pointed toward the private room.

I did as I was told and forty minutes later had a life-changing tattoo centered on my spine. I was secretly delighted and couldn't wait to show Sam. It did make me feel a little younger— maybe it was the spontaneity of it, or maybe it made me feel a little rebellious. I already had one tattoo, an infinity symbol I got many years earlier. I remember thinking at the time that I was such a wild and crazy woman despite my round glasses and professor persona. Little did I know that pretty much every lesbian in the world sported a tattoo of some kind. The new one made me smile, and I thought maybe it really was a symbol of new things to come.

Chapter 3

I got back to the house a little before six. Jack and I were sidetracked in Deep Ellum, checking out some cool vacated buildings. I had this fantasy of renovating something historical in downtown Dallas. Jack was always good about encouraging my dreams, and we both fell in love with an old hat factory. "Sammy? I'm home."

"You're late. I told Jack to have you here by five."

"What happened to 'did you have fun'? Sorry. We were looking at buildings."

"Hi baby." She kissed my cheek. "Did you have fun? What did you do for six hours other than admire architecture?"

"We got lewd, screwed and tattooed." I smirked.

"And a little crude. That's a vulgar statement for a conservative woman."

"I know, right?" I peered over my glasses, hoping she would ask if I was serious about the tattoo. I glanced around the house and saw an array of rainbow colored balloons, crepe paper and extra chairs. I was saddened to see our engagement sofa had been pushed off to the side, but I understood we needed more room for guests.

"I'm about to hop in the shower. You're welcome to join me. The food and drinks are set up in the kitchen and dining room. Andrea didn't show, but I doubt anyone will linger much in the yard."

"That's not like Andrea. She usually calls if she can't come by. Maybe I should track her down." I thought about our young friend who tended the yard, pool and various handyman tasks.

"She's fine, Doc. She left a message and apparently just had her third date with some woman. They're probably out renting a U-Haul and buying puppies as we speak. We need to get dressed and ready before people show. You know Sarah and Jules will be here half an hour early."

"Why do they do that? The invitation says seven, so they deduct half an hour for some space-time continuum?"

"I think they allow for traffic. Jules doesn't understand that it's okay to be late to a party. You know how she is."

"Damn perfectionists," I answered. "Always cutting into my shower time." I stripped off my clothes and casually glanced in the mirror at my new artwork before joining Sam in the shower. I wrapped my arms around her neck and leaned in for a kiss.

"We don't have time, Doc." She practically pushed me away and my mind flashed back to the previous night's conversation. She didn't want me. She didn't want to marry me; she had no desire to even kiss me anymore. That's a hell of a birthday gift, I thought. I took a quick shower and joined her by the sink.

"I know what you're thinking," she said while putting on mascara.

"I really doubt that, Sam." I tried to sound condescending, but it came off as wounded.

"You think I don't want to touch you anymore." She batted her eyelashes and admired the perfection in the mirror.

"You're quite the mind reader, aren't you?" I put spray in my hair and flipped my head forward.

"If it makes you feel better, that artwork on your back is the sexiest thing I've seen in years, despite its puffiness and impending scab. If we weren't expecting a houseful of people in twenty minutes, I would throw you on the bed and kiss every inch of your body." She stared at me in the mirror.

"Well, you're full of surprises today." I blushed and almost wanted to cry from the compliment.

"There's a whole night of surprises ahead, Dani. Get dressed." She buttoned her shirt and patted my hip as she exited the bathroom.

I watched her walk out of the room and couldn't help but

smile. There was something about the way that woman could make a pair of faded jeans and a French-cuffed shirt look like something out of a fashion magazine. I continued to watch as she tucked in her shirt, added some cuff links and slipped into her heels. She must felt me watching her because she turned my direction, undid one more button on her shirt and winked. I melted.

Jules and Sarah were the first to arrive, as expected. Also as expected they brought trays of food. They each had varying degrees of OCD which meant they wouldn't eat certain foods unless they personally saw them being prepared. They also brought me a T-shirt from my old college, perhaps hoping it would encourage my return. I was grateful for the attempt and told them I would consider the option. Jules used to be my teaching assistant and she recently finished graduate school and would soon have an assistant of her own.

Jack arrived next, empty-handed as expected. I was surprised to see that he didn't have a date; he assured me that his people would arrive later. The guests slowly filed in over the next hour and by nine, everyone on the guest list was accounted for. I was happy to be surrounded by my friends. Really I was just happy to feel a little life in the house. The doldrums of being home alone all day, every day were wearing on me. The sound of laughter resonated throughout our historic bungalow and I couldn't have asked for a better gift.

I made a point to walk through the house several times to greet every person and appreciate every ounce of Sam's effort. I was particularly pleased to see so many of my former colleagues in attendance and it made me yearn for my teaching days, but only for a second. I ran into our neighbor and wondered how old Mrs. Johnson could still be alive—she must have been a hundred. All the excitement from living next to a wild woman like Sam should have given her a heart attack years ago. I lingered in the kitchen for a while and enjoyed the smell of all my favorite foods. Sam's hotel caterers really went overboard with all the bar foods that I loved so much but rarely allowed myself to indulge in.

Sam tracked me down while I was on the patio with the smokers, fighting the urge for a cigarette. "Doc, two of your guests want to see you in the living room."

"Send them out here," I whispered. I didn't want to be rude and leave the smokers' conversation. Plus, I was enjoying the second handsmoke.

"Just trust me and go inside, jackass." She pulled the sleeve of my jacket and I followed her into the living room.

Standing by the front door, looking gorgeous and tired, was Toby's wife, Amelia Garcia—Latina songstress, megastar, Sam's sister-in-law, my best friend. "Feliz cumpleanos, chica!"

"Amelia! I don't believe it. I thought you were on tour." I ran into her arms and squeezed her tightly.

"You never check my Web site, do you? My tour dates are still pending." She returned the tight embrace.

I couldn't help but notice her perfume. It always made me think of sunflowers. I tried not to hug her for too long, but it was always hard to let go. Not only was she beautiful and always dressed to the nines in clingy black dresses, but she gave perfect hugs. "Where's Toby? Waiting in the limo for a grand entrance?" I peeked through the curtains.

"He's still in France doing the hotel gig." She sounded apologetic. "But he said to give you a hug and a big kiss on the lips." She kissed my cheek. "I told him the lips belonged to Sam."

"Baby, I thought you said two of my guests wanted to see me."

"Well…" She paused and looked at Amelia.

"Toby and I are having a baby. I'm pregnant, Doc." Her eyes danced as she spoke.

I stood there speechless. My initial reaction was concern for her singing career, but then the goodness of her words struck me. "We're gonna be aunts, Sam!" I jumped up and down.

Tears rolled down her cheeks as if the reality finally set in for her. "I know, baby. I can't wait."

We got Amelia and her vast amount of luggage settled in the guest room so she could rest for a bit while Sam and I went back to entertaining our guests. I was surprised to see that everyone was still there at midnight. I asked Jack where his people were, and he told me that Amelia was his date for the night. Amelia joined the party a little after twelve and Sam gathered everyone in the living room. I tried to act casual, but knew it was time for my big gift. Sam gave the best presents; I knew there was something better than an eBay Atari system.

"I have another gift for Doc." She handed me a big box, much bigger than the one that came in the mail. "Another blast from the past. Happy birthday."

I shook the box side-to-side and admired the perfect wrapping and bright blue ribbon. Finally, I tore open the paper and revealed a Cabbage Patch doll. I tried to hide my disappointment. "You really did hit Wal-Mart last night, eh?" I kept smiling, but had no idea what else to say.

"Check out her name," Sam said, looking nervous.

I opened the little tag attached to the doll's foot that read, My name is Amy. I wasn't sure how to react. It seemed a little strange that she thought a doll named Amy would be a welcomed gift. Everyone in the room stared at me like they knew some secret, so I feigned delight and thanked her. "Wow. That's very thoughtful, Sam. I appreciate the gift." I put the doll back in the box and grabbed my pint glass of warm lager.

Sam retrieved the doll and handed it back to me. "Look in her pocket." A strange look came across her face—a look of fear or nausea. I'd seen that look before when she was nervous about my reaction to something.

I tried to remain calm while glancing around the room at the supportive and excited faces and did as I was told. Inside the front dress pocket were two rings. Both rings were platinum, one with five diamonds, and the other with four. My legs suddenly felt weak and I remembered the box that arrived in the mail. It made sense to me now why she didn't want to discuss the wedding the previous night. She had a plan. Sam always had a plan. Sam always made a grand gesture, no matter how dramatic and corny, she did the right thing.

"Wow." It was the only word I could force through the lump in my throat.

"Dani. Will you finally marry me?" She whispered the words

in my ear like it was a question no one else should hear.

I thought about being sarcastic in my reply. I thought about teasing her and saying no. I knew in my heart that this wasn't a time to be glib, so I whispered back, "Yes."

She took the rings from my hand and placed the one with five diamonds on my finger. She handed the other back to me and held out her hand. I placed the four-stoned ring on her hand. "I love you," she said and put her hand on the back of my neck.

"I love you, too," I replied and kissed her as our friends and family quietly clapped.

Sam turned to the group of onlookers. "Okay, everyone. Last call. We have a big day tomorrow."

"What?" I blushed, then realized I might have blown her cover. She might have been lying to get people to leave so we could consummate our official engagement.

Jack handed me an envelope and winked. "Here ya go, kid." On the outside it read, Happy birthday, Doc. With all our love, Jack, Amelia and Toby. Inside the envelope were two tickets to Amsterdam. "Your flight leaves in five hours, you'd better get packed." He couldn't stop grinning.

"Are you kidding me?" My hands started to shake.

"Don't worry. You aren't getting married on this trip. The three of us decided you two should get over there and scope out a venue for the ceremony. We knew if you didn't leave immediately, you'd put it off for three more years. These are first-class tickets with an open return. We also decided that you should take your time. Come back when you're ready, whether it's three days or three months, take your time and find something perfect." Jack was beaming with excitement.

I looked at Sam in awe. "Is he serious? What about your job?"

"He is serious. I told them about the rings and the three of them brainstormed. They called me Monday with the idea and I juggled my cases and took an open-ended vacation. I've been off since yesterday and have been running all over town for two days getting everything settled."

"What happens if we're gone too long and the firm replaces

you?" I'd already started my "what if" scenarios.

"Then I find another firm, or I focus full-time on the hotel business again. Dani, there is nothing more important to me than our future together. We can afford to be a little frivolous. Don't stand here and debate, go pack some clothes for January in Holland." She pointed toward the bedroom door.

I started to ask the obvious question. "What's th—"

"Winter, baby. Cold," Sam interrupted. "Take sweaters."

I turned to Jack and Amelia. "I can't thank you enough. I feel like this was some sort of intervention. Kind of like we are addicted to marriage procrastination so the family steps in and next thing you know I'm on a plane." I felt stupid for the analogy, but they seemed to understand.

"Just go pack." They both hugged me, still smiling.

"Okay. Thanks for coming," I said to the crowd, not knowing what else to say. I was feeling a little panicked and overwhelmed. I hugged a few people as I went into the bedroom and had an anxiety attack.

Sam joined me in the packing frenzy about twenty minutes later. "Everyone left except Amelia and Jack. They're playing Atari in the den."

"Is this for real, Sam? Are we seriously heading to Holland in a few hours? What about—"

Sam interrupted me again. "Amelia is staying here at the house with Jack until Toby gets back from France, then Toby will stay and Jack can go home. It works out well; Amelia needed an escape and someone to keep an eye on her pregnant self. You know Jack would kill to spend time with Amelia. Everything is taken care of, baby. Stop questioning everything and just prepare for an adventure."

"One more question and I'll shut up," I said.

"One more. Shoot." She smiled.

"I thought you wanted more diamonds. Why didn't you get us the same ring? Why does mine have the extra stone?"

"That extra stone is your reminder that you are the center of my world, Doc." She winked.

I didn't know what to say, so I emptied my sock drawer into a duffle bag and prepared for our adventure.

Chapter 4

Jack dropped us off at Dallas/Fort Worth's international terminal around five a.m. Our nonstop flight was to leave at 6:40 and a mere sixteen hours later we would be landing at Amsterdam's Schiphol airport. I was so excited that the thought of sleep never crossed my mind. I was filled with questions about our trip, even though Sam and I had visited Holland together years earlier.

"So we are leaving today, but we'll arrive there tomorrow?" The question didn't make sense, even to me.

"Yes. Today is Saturday. Consider the plane ride as your Saturday. You went from lunch, to tattoo parlor, to your birthday party, to the airport, to arrive in a foreign country. We aren't staying in a hotel, specifically. One of the chains owns some apartments near the Red Light District. We have a two-story, one bedroom apartment and can check in whenever we want."

"Ouch. I bet that's expensive." I cringed when it occurred to me that the flight alone must have cost five thousand each.

"Actually it was only thirty Euro more per night. There's no room service or security. I think most travelers prefer the safety of a hotel, so the apartments are a great deal for us brave souls. I'm so glad there isn't a Laine Hotel in Amsterdam. I love going on a vacation where I don't have to be a family representative." She sighed.

"Yeah. It'll be nice to see a country without having to deal with people kissing your ass, free limo rides and all that terribleness," I teased. The perks really were nice, but Sam had a way of getting caught up in critiquing the hotels and ignoring the vacation fun. "I guess I get your full attention this time?"

Sam was already asleep.

I busied myself for an hour playing with my PSP and reading the airline magazines. I took full advantage of the first-class seats and slurped down a few Heinekens before they started *Meet The Fockers*, the in-flight movie. It was one I hadn't seen before, so I rested my head on Sam's shoulder and tried to focus. I probably made it through the first scene before I drifted off.

"Doc. Doc, wake up." Sam tugged at my sweater.

I awoke completely discombobulated. It took me a few moments to remember the events of the last twenty-four hours. Finally, I could respond. "What? What's wrong?"

"Nothing. You were snoring like a banshee," she whispered, annoyed.

"Do banshees actually snore? What the hell is a banshee, anyway?" I had a slight headache and was irritated.

"A banshee is a female spirit in Irish mythology." The accented voice came from the seat in front of us.

"Oh." I was caught off guard by the stranger's answer. "Well, do they snore?"

The woman laughed. "Not as loudly as you do."

"Sorry about that. I hope I didn't annoy you," I apologized. "What are they the spirit of?"

"I should lie and say they are a sign of good things to come. Honestly, they are an omen of death." The woman looked at us from between the seats.

"Probably death from sleep apnea." Sam tried to make light of the awkwardness. "I'm Samantha."

"I'm Alma." She looked at me. "It's all good."

"Well, thank you. I'm Dani." I smiled.

"No. I mean my name. Alma means all good," Alma said.

"Oh. Dani means loud snorer." I laughed. "Samantha means awkward stranger."

"Nice to meet you." She turned around as the flight attendant approached our seats with the dinner cart.

The sun was slowly coming up as we taxied into the Schiphol

airport. There wasn't a cloud in the sky and I took that as a sign of good things to come. It was cooler than I thought it would be, even though I had already been told it was winter in the Netherlands. I had forgotten what a beautiful city it was and even simply standing outside the airport gave me a comforting sense of history, even though the airport itself was hardly a historical building.

We took a cab to the hotel that owned the apartments and found no one in the lobby. We looked in the dining room, bar and even the offices. No one.

"Maybe it's siesta time," I remarked.

Sam laughed. "They don't have siestas in the Netherlands."

"Pot is legal here, I bet everyone naps."

"Not if you find the right kind of pot." She climbed up on the counter to see what was on the other side. "Aha. Pssst. Mister, are you awake?" She coughed a few times then repeated herself.

I heard a deep grunt, followed by a squeaky voice. "I'm sorry, long night." The man rose and appeared behind the counter. He had to be the most gorgeous man I had ever seen in my life, with his dark hair, high cheekbones and vibrant blue eyes. "How can I help you?"

"We have a reservation for an apartment. The last name is Laine." Sam must have thought he was striking as well because her eyes were fixed on his. It was the first time I ever worried about her attraction toward a man, and I couldn't blame her.

"Laine. Here it is, checking in Sunday. When do you plan on departing?" His accent was wonderful, as was his English.

"We aren't sure yet. How long is the apartment available?" Sam still stared into his eyes.

"It's booked starting March first, so you have six weeks available." He smiled. "Think you ladies can survive that long?"

"Probably not. How about we plan on two weeks and if we decide to stay longer, we'll let you know."

"Okay, but if you leave early, we need twenty-four hour notice." He was staring back at Sam. "Let me run your card and I'll take you to your home away from home." Sam handed him the credit card and he smiled. "Like the Hotel?"

She looked around then fixed her eyes on the big fountain in the middle of the lobby. "Yes, it's very nice." She sounded casual.

"No. Laine. Like the Laine hotel?" He handed the card back.

It was obvious by her smile that she knew what he meant the first time. "Yes, pronounced the same." She looked at me and rolled her eyes.

We gathered our luggage and followed the beautiful man to an old building three blocks from the hotel. The apartment sat between a restaurant and a bakery and the back overlooked a canal. We had to walk up a narrow flight of curved stairs, which was rather difficult with large bags in tow. It was evident from the crumbling brick and classic architecture that the building was at least a century or two old. The apartment was pretty nice, nothing spectacular, but better than a regular hotel room. The living room had three large windows with the canal view and attached to it was a very small kitchen area. A small room housed the toilet, and another room across the hall had a shower and sink. At the end of that hall a flight of four stairs led up to the bedroom. The view from that window was of the street below. The smell of baked goods wafted from the bakery next door.

The hot hotel guy handed us our keys. "You ladies need to be careful. There is no security here. The key opens your door and the building's door downstairs. Other tenants have the same key. Some are travelers; some are permanent renters who prefer not to be bothered by tourists. The heart of the Red Light District is two blocks over. Just head toward the church and you will start to see it. Have you been to Amsterdam before?"

"Yes, years ago, we were here for a week or so." I couldn't help but stare into his eyes.

"Then you know to be careful. Don't walk the area alone. Do not, under any circumstances, talk to or buy anything from anyone who approaches you on the street. We have coffeehouses if you want anything legal. Street people are not selling legal goods, and they might just be trying to get you to pull out your money. Don't go into any bathroom in public places where you don't have a key."

"What do you mean by that?" I wasn't sure how I would have a key to public bathrooms.

"Lots of places have attendants and charge you for bathroom use. That's fine. If there is no charge, and no one working or sitting outside the facilities, don't just walk in. Most places keep the key to the ladiesroom behind the bar. Ask for the key, and look around before you enter."

I had never heard anything like that before. "Is this a new course of action?"

"We have a lot of tourists here who get drunk and, shall we say, aroused, from the sex shows. Some don't go to the prostitutes and get a little aggressive when they see a pretty woman in a bar. This isn't a law or a policy, it's just some common sense advice. Be careful, this is a wonderful, fun, relatively safe town, but it's always good to be cautious. The locals will be helpful, but keep an eye on the drunken men." He raised an eyebrow. "Is there anything else I can do for you ladies?"

"Leave us a jar of sperm and a turkey baster," I whispered to Sam.

"I'm sorry? What?" He leaned in.

"She asked what your name is," Sam covered.

"Kyler." He handed Sam a card. "If you need anything at all, call this number. Someone is available at the hotel twenty-four hours."

"Thank you, Kyler. Hope to see you again." She handed him some Euro.

The moment we heard him exit the building, I said, "I was serious about the sperm. Can you imagine what beautiful children he'd produce?"

"Imagine it? Hell, honey, I've already named them Kyler Junior and Slapme Silly."

"I'll move him to the top of my list of If I Had to Sleep With Three Men."

"Who are the other two?" Sam asked.

"Duh, Steven Tyler and that guy from Puddle of Mudd."

She laughed. "So you found a replacement for Bill

Clinton?"

"It was just a ploy to get to meet Hillary anyway."

While Sam placed her perfectly starched hanging clothes in the closet, I curled up on the soft king-sized bed and enjoyed the smell of baked goods. I was trying really hard to stay awake, but the scent and the comfort of the bed took over and I fell asleep.

"Wake up, ass." Sam was shaking me. "You know the rule of global travel."

"What rule?" I rolled over and placed my head on her leg.

"You can't succumb to jet lag. You gotta hit the ground running or you'll never adapt to the time difference." She stroked my hair. "Go take a shower and I'll unpack your things for you."

"Wanna shower with me?" I waggled my eyebrows.

"Too small. But I appreciate the offer."

"Too small? I thought size didn't matter." I sniffed.

"Go!" she yelled and pointed toward the door. "And don't fall asleep in there. I know how you are."

I took a long cold shower because I couldn't figure out how the faucet worked. I had never seen two spigots in the shower before, and I was too tired to ponder for too long. When I exited the bathroom, I found that Sam had laid out some clothes for me. I started to get dressed when I realized she had forgotten my panties. I looked through all the bags and all the drawers and found none of my own underthings. "Sam, where are my dainties?"

She burst out laughing as she entered the bedroom. "You tell me, Doc. I think you forgot some necessities."

"What?" I racked my brain and realized that I packed a lot of socks but missed the panty drawer completely. "Shit. What am I gonna do?"

"No big deal, we'll buy some things today and send them to the hotel laundry service." She sounded annoyed, probably because she knew I wouldn't wear new panties unless they were washed.

"Well, I can't wear the same underwear I wore all

day yesterday." I felt stupid that we were even having the conversation.

"Then don't wear panties. I guarantee you won't be the only woman in Holland going pantyless."

The thought of it repulsed me. My other option was to wear a pair of Sam's, and as much as I loved her, that just seemed weird. "I'm not buying underwear in the Red Light District. They probably only sell lace thongs and crotchless teddies."

"My God, woman. How did you get to be such a stick in the mud? We'll walk to the mall. It's less than a mile from here near Dam Square behind the palace." She put on her shoes.

"I don't think I'm a stick in the mud because I don't like to walk around commando." My feelings were a little hurt that she'd said that. I couldn't help that I was raised to dress appropriately at all times. I'm the type who puts on a bra just to take out the trash.

I finished getting dressed and just felt awkward without the extra layer of cotton on my body. I thought about wearing an extra pair of socks to balance things out, but I knew it wouldn't be the same.

Magna Plaza was a magnificent building built in the 1750s. It used to house the main post office, but had been transformed into a wonderful shopping center. I was surprised by the sparseness of the shops. Unlike stores in the U.S. where we cram a million things out in the open, the shops at the Plaza looked bare. For every item they sold, they only displayed one of each size. It kind of made sense, why set out ten size large shirts of the same style? I assumed they restocked the merchandise after you made a purchase. How many people were going to buy two of the same item in the same size? It kind of made me wonder why American stores display so much merchandise. Perhaps they want the consumer to feel a sense of security knowing that lots of items are available. Maybe Americans are too lazy to restock an item after it sells. Perhaps American stores could be smaller, like those in Europe, if they only put out the mandatory display items. Anyway, I found some panties.

We stumbled across a fantastic clothing store that sold my

fantasy wardrobe. Imagine if you could have a personal designer who only made clothes to fit your body and style perfectly. That's the type of store we ventured into. They had cowboy shirts that didn't look like a rancher previously wore them and jeans that didn't have a high crotch or bell bottoms. I was in denim heaven, and I knew I wasn't going to leave empty-handed. Within ten minutes, I had four pairs of jeans and two shirts in my possession.

A mousy voice came from a tall blonde. "Kan ik u helpen?"

"Ik spreek het geen Nederlands." I thought I told her I didn't speak Dutch, but her laugh suggested that I said something stupid. I blushed.

"Can I help you?" She smiled.

"Oh, I think I'll continue to look around." I spotted another treasure out of the corner of my eye.

"Are you familiar with our sizes?" she asked.

"Not really." It hadn't occurred to me to look for my size. Out of excitement, I just grabbed the first thing I saw.

"You should try them on," Sam suggested as she walked toward us.

"Of course, you are welcome to try on anything you want," the saleswoman replied.

"Um." I panicked knowing I was about to open myself up for ridicule. "I can't try on pants today."

Sam started laughing. "Why not? Why can't you try on pants today?"

"You know why," I whispered and elbowed her in the ribcage.

"No I don't." She turned toward the saleswoman. "I have no idea why she can't try on pants today of all days."

"Sam, stop it," I said under my breath while my glasses started to fog up from the heat on my face.

"Stop what, Dani?" She smiled at the saleswoman and rolled her eyes. "Just try them on. You don't want to buy the wrong size." She looked back at me. "You do have extremely long legs. Almost disproportionate." She was really pushing it.

I knew Sam wasn't going to stop until I confessed. I decided to drop the embarrassment and explain. "I can't try on pants today because I'm not wearing any underwear." I was ready for Sam to remind me that I had just bought panties, and I was dreading having to explain in front of a stranger that I refused to wear unwashed underwear.

"I see," said the saleswoman, calmly.

"What! You're not wearing underwear?" Sam shouted loudly enough to get the attention of everyone in the store. "That's disgusting. You should be ashamed of yourself!" She stormed out of the store laughing.

I stood there red-faced, not knowing what to do. Finally I handed the pile of clothes to the woman and said, "I'll be back another time. Thank you." Then I ran from the store and almost knocked over a display case filled with adorable T-shirts that I would have killed for.

Sam was waiting for me by the escalator, her body shaking from giggles.

"Don't talk to me." I walked past her and put my hand beside my eyes like I couldn't even look at her.

"You really need to loosen up." She laughed louder and tried to catch up to me.

I walked a little faster and headed out the door into the street. "You are such an ass."

"Let me make it up to you. What do you want to do? Are you hungry? Thirsty? Wanna get high, little girl?" She was dancing in circles around me, possibly giddy from jet lag.

"I'm kinda hungry," I answered.

"Okay, what do you want?"

I thought for a moment. "Dutch pancakes."

She burst out laughing. "Okay, but only if you promise to order them just like that."

I was missing the joke. "Why?"

"Because here, the Dutch people just call them pancakes."

"That's it. I'm going home." I grabbed my bag of underwear from under Sam's arm and started walking. The paper-handled bag got caught on her watch and split in half. Eight pairs of large cotton granny panties fell to the ground. I did everything I could not to cry. I could see Sam out of the corner of my eye.

She was in silent hysterics.

I dropped my half of the bag and left her. I waited until I was safely around the corner to peek back and watch her on the street picking up my panties. I never laughed so hard in my life. I couldn't wait to marry that woman.

I walked back to the apartment by myself. It was around noon and I did everything I could to stay awake. I was flipping channels on the little TV when I heard something hit the window. I peeked through the glass and saw Sam in a black pea coat standing on the cobblestone sidewalk near the canal.

"Hey!" she shouted. Even though I could hear her, I pointed to my ear and pretended I couldn't. She cupped her hands over her mouth. "Open the window, Doc!"

I cranked the handle and let the cold air enter the room. "What do you want?"

"I don't have a key. I left mine on the coffee table," she yelled.

I looked around and saw the key. "Yes, you're right," I shouted back and started to crank the window closed.

"Doooc! It's cold out here. Come down and open the door." She pretended to shiver.

"I don't have any shoes on. Sorry." I slowly turned the crank, giving her time for one last plea.

She responded, "Damn, woman. First you don't wear panties, now you aren't wearing shoes."

"Have a nice day!" I yelled and closed the window. I sat back down on the sofa. Another stone hit the glass. I held back a smile as I opened the window.

"I'm sorry! You're right, I'm a total ass. You don't have to come down, but could you throw me a key?" People on the street were starting to stare at her.

"Give me one reason why I should let you in. You've been picking on me ever since we landed."

"Because if you don't throw me the key, I'm gonna toss your big cotton panties into this cold dirty canal." She held up the ripped bag.

"Big?" I tried to sound upset. "You think my drawers are

big?"

"No, no. Wait. Your dainty, cute, flowery panties. I'll throw all eight little pair into the water if you don't toss down a key." She still pretended to shiver.

"Um. No, but thanks for playing." I closed the window and sat back down. A minute later I glanced down at the canal and saw a single pair of flowery pink underwear floating on top of the water. She loved to play dirty. I decided the game had gone on long enough, so I grabbed the key and opened the window.

"Gosh, I hope they weren't your favorites." She shouted then pulled another pair from the torn bag.

"You want the key? Here's the key!" I intended to throw it as hard as I could so she would have to walk down the street to get it. Instead my hand hit the window on the follow-through...the key went flying into the canal, splashing next to my floating panties.

Under normal circumstances Sam would have been irritated and I would have felt guilty for doing something so stupid. Perhaps we were giddy from jet lag or the excitement of being on vacation. We took one look at each other and we both burst out laughing. "I'll be down in a second," I said through chuckles.

Chapter 5

We decided it was best to put off the wedding planning until we were well rested and not at war. I wanted to hit the museums, but Sam had other plans for us. "Let's go window shopping."

I knew what she meant, and hoped she wasn't out to make a purchase. "Are we just browsing, or will money be exchanging hands?"

"I don't think they allow girl on girl action in the district, and I have no need to play with others when I already sleep with the woman of my dreams." She was trying hard to redeem herself.

"I appreciate the effort, but your nose is growing. I'll be happy to check out the sights with you. Maybe we can find some bridesmaids for the ceremony."

"I'm sure your parents would love that. As if it isn't bad enough you're marrying a woman, the wedding party consists of prostitutes. We could have the reception in a coffee shop and have a cake made of hash." She pulled on her coat.

"Yeah, my mom probably thinks that hash brownies are the side order to scrambled eggies." I laughed. "I doubt they'll come to Holland anyway. I can't imagine they'd endure a daylong flight to attend a ceremony for a marriage they won't acknowledge." I chewed on a fingernail.

"I'm sure they'll acknowledge the wedding." She tried to reassure me. "They've been great about keeping in touch and being friendly to me."

"That's all well and good until we visit them in their little safe haven. We'll be given separate rooms and you will be introduced as Dani's friend the lawyer."

"That's better than Dani's friend the asshole," she retorted. "Get your coat, no talk of families or lawyers today."

"You know, some people think lawyers and assholes are the same thing." I grabbed my coat. "Do you have a key this time, or will we be dragging the canal at two in the morning?"

"I got the key. You know, Doc, I'm not so sure you'd be comfortable if your parents introduced me as your girlfriend or your wife anyway. You don't show me any affection when they visit. When they were at our house for Christmas last year, you and I became roommates and you barely kissed me goodnight even when we were alone. Their presence sends you straight back to the closet."

She made a good point. "So do you think they'd accept you as my wife if I kissed you at the dinner table?" I thought for a moment. "Maybe I should grope you under the mistletoe." The thought of doing that in front of my parents gave me the willies. I could picture their faces and practically hear my mom's feet running from the room.

"No, I'm just saying maybe if you didn't treat me like a roommate, they might not think of me as just a friend." She ran her fingers through her blonde hair.

"O'Connors aren't affectionate people. Public displays of affection are taboo, whether between parent-child, husband-wife or even wife and wife." I sighed.

"That sounds weird." Sam lifted an eyebrow. "Wife and wife. The thought of being a wife is such a foreign concept for me. The thought of having a wife seems surprisingly natural though. I wonder why that is."

"Because you're gay. We gals who love gals want a woman at home—a wife. But the stereotypical wife is a cooker, cleaner, baby-maker. So those of us who aren't the soccer mom type don't ever think of being stereotypical."

"So you want a wife, but don't want to be a wife. I want a wife, but don't want to be a wife. We have a lot in common, but shouldn't one of us at least commit to being a cooking, cleaning, baby-maker?" she asked.

"Wow, this is deep. We may need some hash brownies," I said.

"Okay, but no scrambled eggies. Then we'd have to have the whole chicken and egg conversation."

"Same conundrum, different species."

As we walked the cobblestone streets of Amsterdam, I felt an unusual sense of peace. Perhaps it was because of the reason we were on the trip, perhaps it was because the city itself is so beautiful and rich in history. I had the sudden urge to hold Sam's hand. I wasn't sure if it would be weird, then as we rounded the corner, I saw two other women coming out of a bar holding hands. That was the only sign I needed. I placed my hand in Sam's and she squeezed mine tightly. "There ya go, baby. A little public display of affection never hurt anyone." She smiled.

"Let's get a beer." The pastries we had from the bakery earlier had finally settled and I was ready to start loosening up.

"Where? There's a regular bar there." Sam pointed across the street. "Then there's a bar and sex show over there. And I think we passed a lesbian bar on the last block."

"How do you know it was a lesbian bar?" I knew I was setting her up.

"Because it had a Superman tattoo, and was wearing a flannel shirt and Doc Martens."

"Good one. You're really on a roll today. I don't care where we go as long as they have Grolsch on tap." For some reason that particular lager never gave me a hangover.

"There's a Grolsch sign at the end of the alley. Let's check it out." She pulled me down a narrow stone path.

When we entered the bar, I knew we were in for an adventure. There were no windows, so it felt like three in the morning the instant we sat down on our barstools. Neon signs lit up the bar area and the sweet cigar stench was enough to make you vomit. There was a small stage in the middle of the bar, and little tables surrounding it. Of the handful of patrons scattered throughout the little tables, the majority of them were men in their seventies wearing bad toupees and muscle shirts. I guessed they were probably German, but I didn't care to find out. "Let's go somewhere else, Sam. This looks a little weird."

"Where's the brave soul who took my hand on the street? Where's the crazy lady who tossed my room key in the canal?" She tried to get the bartender's attention.

"Okay, the key thing was an accident." I stood up just as the bartender approached.

"U wilt bier?" he asked while wiping the counter.

"Ja. Twee. Grolsch." Sam traveled a lot and made it a point to learn some simple phrases. She was able to order beer in seven languages, and she could ask for the bathroom in over twenty countries.

"Very impressive," I said. "Now let's pay the man and leave." I turned toward the door.

"Sit down and relax. We're perfectly safe. There are some other ladies here." She motioned toward the back of the bar. "See, over there."

I glanced over my shoulder and saw the women she was referring to. "Yeah. They're naked, Sam." I tugged on her jacket to indicate that we, on the other hand, were fully dressed.

"So? This coming from a woman who probably still isn't wearing underpants?" She made the statement just as the bartender returned with our beer.

"Thanks," I whispered and blushed. She knew they weren't back from the hotel laundry yet.

"He doesn't speak English. It's cool," she assured me.

"That'll be three Euro, cash only ladies." He laughed. "Two Euro for you and one for the lady with no underpants."

I flipped a coin onto the bar. "Dank u."

"This would be a nice place for a reception. We could set up a buffet on the stage and bring in a deejay." She pretended to take notes.

"Please stop making light of everything. We're supposed to be here planning our future, not getting drunk in nudie bars."

"It was your idea to get drunk, panty-less." Loud music suddenly blasted from the speakers and I couldn't hear what she said next, although I'm sure it contained more sarcasm.

As soon as the music started, the naked women from the back of the bar walked toward the stage. On the way they stopped and said hello to the old men, like they had known them for years. I imagined they were probably regulars. Before they stepped up to the stage, one of them looked our way and waved. I couldn't help but smile and wave back. "She's pretty." The woman walked toward me while doing a little dance. I felt a little anxious about how I was supposed to react, so I continued to smile and felt my face grow hot.

"You Americans?" she asked while rubbing herself on my leg.

"Yes." I put my hands to my side and looked to Sam to save me.

"You're on your own, Doc." She handed me some cash.

I knew in topless bars, you were supposed to put the cash in their panties. I had no idea what to do with the money when the women were, well, panty-less. "Nice tattoos." I said as I held out the bills. "This is for you." I felt stupid. Obviously the money was for her.

"Dank u, Doc." She winked at me and slowly pulled the cash from my fingers. "Enjoy your walkabout."

"Australian?" I asked as she turned away.

"Oh, pretty and smart. I like American women." She walked to the stage and started dancing around a pole with the other girls.

"Now can we go?" I asked, trying not to smile too much.

"Um. Yeah. I'm suddenly ready for bed."

I looked at my watch. "It's not even six o'clock."

"Good." She winked and I knew what she meant.

Monday was pretty much useless. Sam woke up with a bit of a head cold and I was just flat out exhausted. I realized I had been running nonstop for days, starting with lunch with Jack and ending with an Australian humping my leg and Sam humping the rest of me. We spent the entire day in the apartment eating pastries from the bakery downstairs, watching TV and napping off and on. Normally, I'd be furious to waste a day of vacation, but since we had no determined agenda, I found it exhilarating to be a couch potato in a foreign land…to an extent.

By three o'clock, I was going stir-crazy and the sounds from below made me want a little excitement. "Let's go somewhere." I rested my head on Sam's shoulder.

She sneezed. "I'm not going anywhere. Get me a tissue."

I handed her the roll of toilet paper. "Woman cannot live on pastry alone."

"Some do. The women who look like muffins. I'm sure many women would love to have a diet of baked goods."

"Well, I need some protein to battle the carbs." I showed her my bloated belly.

"Why don't you write something? You're surrounded by inspirational sights. Pick a topic and write a short story." It was apparent she wasn't going anywhere.

"Do you care if I walk around a bit? I'll bring us back some real food and some cold medicine."

"Take the key." She fluffed the sofa pillow. "Please be back before dark so I don't worry that you ran off with the dry-humping Australian."

"Yes ma'am. Do you want anything special?"

"Some real Kleenex. Aspirin and a little hash." She flashed a crooked smile.

"You want hash? We don't even know how to smoke it." Her request surprised me, yet left me a little exhilarated.

"You need some inspiration. I know how to smoke it. I was young once."

"Once. You're still young. I'll see what I can find." I pulled on my coat and headed toward the door.

I didn't have to walk very far to find some great little shops—a butcher, a florist and a pharmacy. I decided to find the hash first so I didn't have to walk around with groceries. It didn't take long to stumble upon a coffee shop. A coffee shop in Amsterdam sells soft drugs. Order this kind of hash in American coffee shops, you will be arrested. Here, I walked into a shop called Rasta Roast and wondered if the term roast was a play on coffee or a reference to getting baked. I tried to explain to the guy behind the counter what it was that I was after. He didn't seem to understand what I was saying, so he handed me a menu that was completely indecipherable to me. On Sam's and my previous trip to Amsterdam, we didn't get very wild and crazy, so I was amazed to see how many options there were when it came to buying drugs. I perused the menu, trying to figure out what kind of high we were after. There was a category for different types of stuff that would make you mellow, goofy, hungry, sleepy or even crazy. It seemed as though one could take multiple kinds of hash and turn into any of the seven dwarfs. The menu offered light hash, dark hash, Moroccan, Afghani and even Nepalese hash. My mind was spinning…either from reading the menu, or from the contact buzz I might have gotten from the smoke floating around me.

I must have looked completely lost because a tall, hippie-looking woman came up and said in an American accent, "Tell me what you're after, sweetheart, and I'll tell you what you need."

"I'm really not sure. Hash." I continued to stare at the menu.

"You strike me as someone who wants something subtle, mellow and light. You're a first-timer, aren't you?" She looked me up and down then patted my arm.

"Yes. That sounds about right." I reached for my wallet.

She glanced around the room. "You can't pay me here. What kind of place do you think this is? You'll have us all arrested."

"Oh, I'm sorry." I put my wallet back in my coat pocket and stared at the floor.

"I'm totally kidding. How much do you want?" From behind the counter, she pulled a box that was filled with what looked like little bricks.

"That's so not funny. Just enough for two people."

"Enough for two. Aren't you sweet. Sorry I messed with you. I'm from the States myself, and I love making the other Americans freak out." She placed a brick in a small plastic bag. "I promise this is very mild and mellow. You're gonna love it. That'll be ten."

I handed her the Euro and took the bag. "Thank you. I'm sure I'll be back."

"Oh, sweetheart, I know you'll be back often. Enjoy." She held up two fingers to indicate peace and smiled.

I couldn't believe I was going grocery shopping with drugs in my pocket. I couldn't believe I was in a foreign country with drugs in my pocket. I bought fresh ground coffee, chocolate bars, a few sodas and cold medicine. I stopped by the floral shop and bought a single flower of some type that I'd never seen before. I tried to ask the chubby red-faced florist what kind it was, but she looked confused. I figured she was stoned, so I paid and left.

I got back to the apartment and found Sam sitting by the window in pajamas staring down at the canal. "Looking for my panties? Did the key surface?"

"No. Listen." She cranked open the window.

I heard the sound of men singing in a foreign language. "What is that?"

"Well, there are two boats. The best I can tell is that it's two competing rugby teams singing their fight songs. They've been going back and forth for ten minutes. They have kegs on the boats, so it may be an interesting battle of music."

"I brought you a flower. I have no idea what it is." I held up the vase.

"It's a tulip. Very nice. You do realize it's plastic, right?"

"I wondered why there was no water in the vase." I set the flower on the table and unpacked the bags.

"Are you high?" she asked.

"Not yet." I pulled the bag of hash from my coat pocket and set it on the coffee table.

"Okay, I have an idea. Go get a pen and paper, and you can write a story about the first time you ever smoked hash."

"That'll be one to put on the annual Christmas letter." I pulled some paper from the desk drawer. "Grandma will be so thrilled."

"Grab a pin from one of my dry cleaned shirts, a coaster and a glass from the bathroom." She was still watching the rugby players below.

I did as I was told, feeling like I was on some sort of weird scavenger hunt. "Anything else?"

"Come sit by me." She patted the chair next to hers. She

took the pin and poked it through the cardboard coaster. Next she attached one brick of the hash to the tip of the pin and set the device down on the coffee table. It kind of looked like an opened, broken umbrella sitting with the handle up. Finally she set the glass upside down over the top of the coaster. "Please tell me you bought a lighter."

"I didn't even think of it." I laughed.

"I know you have one in your luggage. You're still a closet smoker, don't deny it and go fetch."

"I—" I started to argue, but knew she would win. I retrieved the lighter and noticed that my favorite cartoon, *Life with Louie*, was on the TV. "Cool, it's in English."

"Here's what you do, Dani. Lift up the glass, light the hash, and set the glass back down. Let the smoke fill the glass for a minute, then tilt the glass and inhale the smoke from the side." She slid the concoction toward me. "Take a hit and start writing something."

I took the glass and did exactly as she said. "I don't feel anything," I said as I exhaled the sweet smoke after holding it in a moment.

"Really? It's supposed to affect you in the first ten seconds. This must be a defective product." She rolled her eyes and reached for the glass, taking a hit for herself.

"You want a soda?" I walked to the kitchen. "I also got some Dutch chocolate."

"Did you call it that? Did you say please give me some Dutch chocolate to the Dutch salesman?"

"You gotta let some things go, man. No more jokes about Dutch pancakes or panties." I handed her a chocolate bar and she declined.

"Did you just call me man?" She laughed. "Start writing."

I took the paper and pen and sat on the sofa. The rugby players' singing had been replaced by a mariachi band on the canal and *Life with Louie* was still on the TV. The following is exactly what I wrote the first time I smoked hash in Amsterdam:

5:17 p.m.—just took four or five hits of hash from a pin.

5:23 p.m.—seems to have no effect on me whatsoever. Perhaps I should take another hit.

5:25 p.m.—*Life with Louie* is the greatest show ever. They should have left it on the air. Still don't feel anything though.

5:33 p.m.—mariachi music is amazing. I should buy a trumpet. I played the trumpet in junior high, I was pretty good. Not as good as that guy though. Why are they playing mariachi music in Holland? I should investigate.

5:42 p.m.—Sam is a beautiful woman. I should tell her that more often. I really love her. I wonder if she thinks I'm sexy. I'm gonna call her. Wait, she's right there. Never mind.

5:48 p.m.—this chocolate is amazing. I'm not gonna call it Dutch anymore. We're in Dutch, so it won't make sense. I like the way it melts in my mouth. I wish I had some milk, or a beer, or vodka. I can feel my toes. I like toes.

5:55 p.m.—I can't understand a damned word of the TV. I think I'm fucked up. Wait, my show's over. It's the local news… in Dutch. I'm okay. They're fucked up.

6:42 p.m.—just woke up. Someone ate all my chocolate.

That's all I wrote. By seven thirty I was feeling great and in the shower. We had dinner at a restaurant in the hotel and were in bed by ten. I slept a beautiful dreamless sleep and felt incredibly refreshed the next morning.

Chapter 6

By Thursday, Sam's little cold had turned into the full-blown flu. She was miserable and I did everything I could to keep her entertained while we were stuck in the apartment. From tap dancing in wooden shoes, to reading *The Diary of Anne Frank* out loud, I did what I could to make her forget she was sick on vacation. She didn't seem to appreciate any of my gestures and quickly grew irritated with me. On Friday, she pretty much kicked me out, telling me to go be a tourist and stay away as long as possible. I tried not to sulk while grabbing my things and promising I would be home before dark. She said she wasn't worried, which hurt my feelings. I decided to spend the day doing every sinful thing I could think of.

I couldn't decide whether to stay close or venture far, so I walked around a bit and eventually found myself standing outside Centraal Station. I would have to say that the station has to be one of the most beautiful public transportation buildings in the world. It's fully adorned with reddish brick with white painted accents, clocks, and an amazing roof design that even housed statues. I didn't really understand how the bus routes were laid out, and I didn't know where I wanted to go. I figured it was better to hop a bus than a train so I didn't get too far out. I heard an American couple talking about going to the Van Gogh museum, so I followed them and hoped they knew what they were doing. I enjoyed the bus ride and was awed by the number of black Mercedes cabs and bicycles in the city. I wondered how many accidents occurred every day between the two. After about ten stops, I heard the driver shout something that sounded like Van Gogh, so I looked to the American couple and exited as they had.

The Van Gogh museum was larger than I expected. I wondered how many paintings Vincent had actually done in his life to justify such a large hanging space. I wandered around the gift shop for a bit, hoping the crowds for the tour would slow. More and more people came in, so I decided to just buy a ticket and proceed on my own. I was amazed by the variety of people wanting to see Van Gogh. I'd bet that every country and every walk of life was represented from Irish punks in leather jackets to nuns, there was even a group of Jamaican guys with dreadlocks. It was difficult to see the work because of the vast amount of people, so I just hung out in the back and jumped up and down when I wanted to see something. After a while, I started jogging through the museum, past all the work, jumping here and there. I really only cared to see *Starry Starry Night* anyway. I made it past every canvas on every floor in about twenty minutes. It was not very enjoyable, but I was glad I could at least say I did it. No, I never saw his ear.

I felt bad for not calling the apartment to check on Sam, but I would have felt worse if I woke her up. I've learned over the years that when she's sick you either get sick too or stay the hell away. This was a stay away day, so I walked next door to the Rijksmuseum which was mainly filled with art from the Dutch masters. I was reminded of old-time liquor or tobacco ads, and wasn't inspired to do much more than just drink and smoke. I took a picture of the cow sculpture outside the museum then headed down the street. I stumbled across the Hard Rock Café, and thought an American style burger sounded good, but they weren't open yet. I guess people don't eat a lot of burgers at eleven in the morning, even when drugs are legal. I was going to check out some of the nearby shops when I noticed a casino across the street. It was a no-brainer for me, I could spend money on useless souvenirs, or I could experience losing Euros in a foreign country. Who needs another damn T-shirt? I went in, signed in—which is policy here, and I still have no idea why—and fifteen minutes later was comfortably seated behind a Lucky Seven slot machine. Okay, so seven wasn't so lucky for me, but a few other machines hit. I avoided the table games because maybe the language difference would hurt me. Maybe the gesture for "hit me" at the blackjack table might mean something completely different in Holland. I stayed at the casino until around two and walked out into the bright sunshine with an extra two hundred Euros in my pocket.

I did finally make it over to the Hard Rock and enjoyed the hamburger I'd craved all morning. I gagged a little at the amount of mayonnaise that came with the fries, but was delighted to have something that reminded me of home. I enjoyed the fact that the cafes were similar throughout the world, yet each had its own little difference. The best part of the Hard Rock in Amsterdam, for me, was the amazing view of the streets, and Jimi Hendrix's acoustic guitar. It was still only four o'clock by the time I had toured the rock-and-roll memorabilia, so I decided to walk around for a while. I stumbled across a little market area with vendors selling everything from shoes to art to henna tattoos. Since my new tattoo still hadn't healed, I opted to skip the henna one. I found a cool pair of boots that would have cost twice as much in America. I didn't buy them because I didn't want to drag them around. I made a mental note to come back with Sam when she was feeling better—she loved shoe bargains. I guess even wealthy people appreciated the hunt. There were a few tourist places I wanted to see like the homomonument, and the Anne Frank Huis. I decided to wait for Sam on those adventures as well because everything is more memorable when you see it with someone else. It occurred to me that on our last trip we spent so much time in the hotel room that we didn't really get out and do much. I hoped we would stay long enough this time to take it all in. We had been in Holland six days and still hadn't made plans for the ceremony, but Sam's being sick was a better excuse than any we had before.

I must have walked circles around the city because my feet were exhausted and the air grew colder. Around seven, I found myself standing below a rainbow flag and turned around to find a cute little girl bar. I mean this as a cute little bar for girls, not a bar for cute little girls, although when I went in, either meaning would have made sense. There was a row of pub tables toward the front and a huge oak bar in the back. The bar itself was lined with a dozen or so beautiful women. It must have been early because the rest of the place was empty. I bellied up to the bar and ordered myself a Heineken because the sign on the door said "Coldest Heineken in Holland." I was not disappointed, they must have kept the keg on ice.

"Hello, vreemdeling." The remark came from a girl to the right of me and all the other bar patrons laughed.

I had no idea what the joke was, so I smiled and held my head down. "Hello."

"American?" the girl asked.

I looked up and noticed that she looked a little like Cameron Diaz, only a bit shorter and stockier.

"Yes." I took a long sip of my drink and prayed she spoke English so I wouldn't be the butt of jokes all evening.

"Do you know what kind of bar this is?" Her accented English was adorable.

"I'm no stranger to bars like these." I assumed she meant gay bars.

"You're a stranger to us? Not many tourists venture in this early?" Every sentence she spoke sounded like a question, like she was trying to confirm she was using the right words.

I fought the compulsion to answer like she had asked a question and just smiled and said, "I see."

"What brings you here?"

I realized that was indeed a question. "I saw that they offer the coldest Heineken in Holland, I had to see for myself."

"No, what brings you to our city?" She moved closer.

I wasn't sure if I should tell her I was planning my wedding because she would think I was stepping out on my girl. "Vacation. Just getting away from it all."

"Well, you picked the right place to escape. I'm Marjolein." She held out her pale delicate hand.

"I'm Dani." I returned the hand gesture.

"Donny. Nice to meet you?"

I started to correct her, but decided it wasn't necessary. I liked the way it sounded coming from her lips. "Nice to meet you too."

We sat in silence for a while and I drank two more small glasses of beer. She talked to her friends in Dutch and I took that as a cue that I wasn't welcome in their conversation. I had asked for my tab when she leaned over to me. "You're not leaving are you?"

"Yes, I should find my way home." It occurred to me that I had no idea how to get back to the apartment.

"Where are you staying?"

"Honestly, I can't remember. I'm in an apartment that belongs to a hotel next to a bakery near the Red Light District." I blushed at my own stupidity.

"That's a pretty far walk from here?"

"I can take a cab," I assured her and myself.

"Not if you don't know where you're going?" she stated or asked, I wasn't sure. "Come dancing with us? There's a private garage a few blocks from here, only the locals know about it. There will be thousands of us there?"

Again I wasn't sure if she was asking or telling. The thought of dancing appealed to me. I thought about calling to ask Sam, but she did imply that she wasn't worried about what I did. "Okay. I'll go with you?" I made it sound like a question intentionally.

"Yes, you will?" She was confusing me.

"Okay then." I paid my tab and waited for her and her friends to finish their drinks.

"Donny, this is Gaby and Tanja." She pointed to the other girls while I smiled.

"What do you do in America, Dani?" Gaby asked, pronouncing my name correctly.

"I used to teach. I took some time off to write a book."

"A Poem for Sam?" She smiled.

My heart started racing. I couldn't believe someone was actually familiar with my little novel. "Yes, actually. Did you read it?" I tried to sound casual.

"I thought you looked familiar from the book jacket. I read it a few months ago. So where's Sam tonight?" She hadn't said whether she liked it.

"She's back at the apartment with the flu. I was told to be

a tourist for the day." I didn't bother to pursue asking what she thought of my writing.

"Okay. Dani's off limits, Marjolein. She has a sick girl at home." Gaby patted me on the shoulder.

"I'm studying to be a doctor?" she asked, or stated. "Does she need help?"

"I think she'll survive. I think my annoying her is worse than the illness itself." I laughed.

"Come annoy us for awhile and we will help you find your way back later." Tanja took my hand and led me out to the street.

I felt a little guilty about the hand holding. I wasn't a very affectionate person, but knew that Tanja's gesture was completely innocent. I secretly enjoyed the feeling of freedom, but wished Sam were there to meet my new friends. "It's cold," I said as we entered the night air.

"I'll keep you warm?" Marjolein said and took my other hand. I felt like a child on her way to get schooled.

The garage was really a three-story warehouse in some industrial district I hadn't walked to that day. We paid a twenty Euro cover and walked into the crowded, loud dance area. The three girls were immediately greeted by a group of trendy, young people. Only one introduced himself—I assumed the others didn't speak English. "I'm Guy. We are all medicals together." He gave me a squeeze. His English wasn't great, but definitely better than my Dutch. He led me to a group of tables in a dark corner where everyone was keeping their drinks and coats while they danced. "Sit down. I'll get you a drink."

I handed him a handful of coins, not knowing how much a pint would cost. "Grolsch?" I found myself asking questions instead of stating facts.

"Grolsch?" he asked.

"Yes," I answered.

"Yes?" he asked.

I felt like we were starting some sort of 'Who's on First?' routine, so I just nodded and he left. I saw Marjolein walking toward me. "This is a neat place," I told her.

"Neat?"

Here we go again. "Yes. Neat. It's a cool place to dance."

"Are you still cold?" She laughed. "I can still make you warm?"

I decided to pretend the music was too loud so I didn't have to play the question game. I pointed to my ears and rolled my eyes. She took my hand and started for the dancing area. "I don't think I shou—" I realized that dancing was easier than talking.

We danced for a solid hour before my feet started to give way. I tried to explain to my new friends that I was tired from walking the stone streets all day. They thought I was asking to get stoned. It took about five minutes to clarify and I was practically in hysterics from laughter and frustration by the time that question-answer conversation was over. I left them on the dance floor and joined Guy and Gaby in a dark corner. They seemed to be fighting, but I couldn't tell. They might have simply been shouting over the music. "May I join you?" I asked and reached for a chair.

"Sit." Gaby pulled out the chair next to her.

"I really should get going," I said as I slammed down one of the five beers in front of me. It seemed that every one of my new friends had bought me a Grolsch.

"Wait for Marjolein. She will get you home; she knows the town better than anyone." Guy smiled as if there was a joke behind the statement. "Here." He handed me a cigarette package.

They were Marlboro Lights, but had large black writing on the side. "What does this mean?" The words appeared to be pretty simple for a surgeon general's warning like the one we have on American cigarettes.

"Basically it says if you smoke these you will die." Gaby pointed to the words while she explained.

"Wow. You guys don't mess around here." I was surprised by the bluntness, but took one anyway, knowing I shouldn't. Guy lit my cigarette and after one drag I was hooked again. The tobacco seemed more pure or clean than what I was used to. "Are these regular cigarettes? They seem very mild."

"Yes. Do you have any? We like American cigarettes. They taste ugly." Gaby laughed.

I kind of knew what she meant. I decided from then on I would only smoke in Europe. I didn't want ugly cigarettes to cause my death. "I don't have any. Sorry."

Marjolein returned from the dance floor and practically sat in my lap. "Are you having fun, Donny?"

I finished another beer. "I'm having a great time, thank you."

"Drink your beers and I will get you back to your apartment near the bakery?" She stroked my hair and handed me a glass.

I looked down to see that someone had set five more small glasses in front of me. I still didn't feel drunk, so I decided not to argue. "Okay, no problem." I slammed the first two and thought I was going to puke. Gaby lit another cigarette for me, but this time it was hand-rolled, and probably not tobacco. I took a hit and felt better.

Marjolein took a hit of the joint, leaned toward me and placed her lips against mine. At first I thought she was kissing me, and then I realized she was passing smoke. I inhaled through my mouth and felt her hand on the back of my neck. I let the smoke out through my nose and she pulled me back and kissed me hard on the mouth. I started to push her away then felt a little tingly. I wasn't sure if it was the beer, the smoke or the softness of her lips, so I relaxed and gave in to the kiss. I heard someone yell her name so we stopped. "Marj!"

"What?" My friend seemed annoyed as she wiped off her mouth. She and some strange woman argued in Dutch for a few minutes.

I started laughing, thinking Ooh, she's in dutch. That's when I realized I was either drunk or stoned and knew I had to leave before the kissing led to something regrettable. "I should go," I said to the group.

Marjolein grabbed my face and kissed me again. Then she pushed me away and looked at the strange woman like she was proving a point. I felt a bit weak in the knees, the kiss was abrupt, and strong, and flat-out erotic. I wanted more, but didn't let on. "I'll take you home." Marjolein took my hand, and waved to the group. Everyone said good-bye in unison and we headed out into the street.

"Where's your car?" I asked as we rounded the corner and entered a dark alley.

"I don't have a car?" she asked or stated as she squeezed my hand.

It occurred to me that I might have put myself in a dangerous situation. I was alone in a foreign country with a perfect stranger. I had no idea where I was staying and Sam had no idea where I was or whom I was with. "It's a bit cold for a long walk. Maybe we should call a cab?" I asked or stated, at that point I wasn't sure.

"Just trust me. You're in for the ride of your life." She walked toward the canal, pulling me behind.

For a moment I thought she was going to push me in. Maybe she thought we could swim back. Soon, I noticed a bank of old fashioned looking bikes. I breathed a sigh of relief. "Which one's yours?"

"Doesn't matter, really. I came on this one." She pulled a bike off the fence and pointed to the book rack on the back.

"Are you serious? You want me to ride on the book rack?" I was starting to sober up quickly.

"It's either that or the handlebars. You're kind of tall and I'd like to see where I'm going?" she asked or stated.

I did as she indicated and straddled the back of the bike. She sat still for a moment, so I wrapped my arms around her body and she pushed off with her feet. A minute later, we rounded the corner onto a cobblestone side street and headed toward the Red Light District. "You were right, Marjolein. This is the ride of my life," I shouted as the cold wind hit my face. I felt her laugh but she didn't respond.

We rode up and down bumpy streets. I don't think she took a direct route, because we passed the Anne Frank Huis and the mall, which were away from the district. Eventually we came across Centraal Station and I knew we were almost to our destination. Just as I saw the hotel, I felt a little disappointment knowing that the journey was almost over. "I bet that's your apartment over there?" she shouted or asked.

"Yes. The building next to the bakery," I answered and couldn't stop smiling. Part of me was glad to be home to Sam, and part of me was exhilarated from just having had the most incredible tour ever. How many Americans get to see the city at night from the book rack of an old-fashioned bike? "Thank you so much. That was the greatest ride I've ever been on," I said as she wheeled up to the building.

"I want to make love to you?" she stated or asked.

I didn't know how to respond. If it was a statement, I was flattered and would of course have declined. If it was a question, my initial response would have been Yes, you do. Of course, I would have remembered that Sam was waiting for me, so I would have laughed and declined anyway. I decided to take it as a statement. "That would be amazing, but my partner is waiting up for me. I could never do anything to hurt her, but I'd like to thank you for a wonderful time tonight. I will remember this ride for the rest of my life. Maybe I'll even write about it one day."

She helped me off the bike and steadied me until I got my land legs back. "You're quite welcome? I enjoyed meeting you? You have a lucky woman upstairs?" She leaned in and gave me a soft slow kiss.

"Thank you." I turned toward the door. "Are you okay to get home?"

"I'm four blocks from here?" She pushed off with her feet and headed down the cobblestone street. I watched her until she rounded the corner and I heard her ring the bell on her handlebars.

It took me several minutes to make my way up the stairs—my ass was already sore from the ride and I knew I wouldn't be walking much the next day. As I entered the apartment, I found Sam awake and drinking a beer. "Hello." I smiled. "You're feeling better."

"Are you asking me or telling me?"

I laughed. "I have no idea."

Chapter 7

"Are you ever gonna get up?" A pillow bounced off my head.

I opened my eyes and realized I had spent the night on the sofa. "What time is it?"

"Almost ten. I've been trying to wake you up for an hour. I've already been to the bakery." She held up a cup of coffee and motioned to a plate of pastry on the table. It was good to see her out of her pajamas and wearing a black fisherman's sweater, tight jeans and boots.

I closed my eyes again and thought of the previous night's events. "How did I end up on the sofa?"

"You came in, said four words to me then lay down on the sofa. You were snoring within three minutes." She sipped her coffee and took a deep breath. "So, what's her name?"

"Whose name?" I panicked, wondering if I had talked in my slumber.

"Oh, don't even try to play coy with me, Doc." Her face was red.

"I'm not playing coy, I just got caught off guard." I should have chosen my words more carefully.

"Got caught? That's pretty accurate. You came in after two in the morning, you could barely walk and you have a hickey on your neck."

My mind raced. "I have a hickey?"

"See? If there wasn't someone you would have denied it. You're such an ass. Did you sleep with someone?"

"Of course not, baby." I laughed at the thought.

"Don't call me baby. Did you meet someone who could have possibly given you a hickey?" She squinted her eyes and tightened her lips.

I put my hand on my neck. "Do I really have a hickey?"

"No. But I can see I've opened a can of worms with the accusation. You'd better start talking, sister, I was worried sick."

"You said you weren't worried as to when I came home. I thought you wanted me to stay out of your hair." I tried to move but my butt was sore. I remembered the bicycle ride and tried not to smile.

"Of course I worried. When you left here, I didn't think you'd reappear eighteen hours later, drunk and smelling like perfume."

"I smell like perfume?" I pulled my shirt to my nose.

"Dammit, Doc! You're not helping your case. If it wasn't a possibility, then why are you sniffing?" She sounded like she was going to cry, but her face didn't show it.

"Sammy. I promise I didn't sleep with anyone. I went to some museums, a casino, the Hard Rock Café and a little lesbian bar. I met some local women there who took me dancing in a warehouse. I didn't know how to get back, so one of the girls gave me a ride home on the back of her bike. That's why I was walking funny." I was careful about how I phrased my response.

"So, what was her name?" She sat down.

"Marjolein. She's a medical student who lives a few blocks from here."

"You always did like the students." She laughed. "Did you kiss her?"

"She kissed me. Honestly, baby, I didn't really reciprocate, but I didn't push her away either. I got caught up in the drugs, booze, excitement and romance of it all."

"It was romantic?" Her voice rose.

"The romance of the city. I gotta tell ya, riding on the back of a Dutch girl's bike through the stoned streets of Amsterdam at one in the morning on a cold winter's night is pretty darned romantic." I couldn't help but smile.

"I could see that." She sipped her coffee. "So you kissed her.

Was it a good kiss?"

"It wasn't bad, kinda sexy. I didn't feel the electricity like I do when you kiss me though."

"Did you exchange information? Are you gonna see her again?"

"No. I don't even know her last name. And if I did see her again, I would introduce you and ask her to give you a ride on her bike." I hoped she would see I had no interest in the woman.

"You know we can't keep kissing other people if we're going to be married."

"I know. Consider it my bachelorette party. I will never get caught up in the moment again with anyone other than you." I waited for a response and she stared at me. "Are you mad?"

"A little. I'm stuck here sick as a dog and you're out having a romantic night with a stranger. I think I'm entitled to be a little pissed, a little jealous and a little sad."

"Sad?"

"You have an amazing experience with someone else. How can I compete with that?"

"Sam, I have amazing moments with you all the time. I don't get out much. So I had fun with a stranger. So I kissed her. I still plan on spending my life with you. All my moments with you mean more to me than anything I could ever have with anyone else. I'll take listening to you talk about work over a drunken night with a Dutch girl any day. Please forgive me." I almost cried when I realized I had made her sad.

"You're on probation. I'm milking this for all I can. I expect my ass to be kissed for the next twenty-four hours. My ass, Dani. Not Marjolein's. Those lips of yours belong to me. Get up, get showered and take me around this town you are now so familiar with."

"You're feeling better."

"You asked me that last night. Or maybe you told me. Yes, I feel fantastic." She smiled.

I went on to tell her about my adventure: the museum, the casino and my new friends. She thought it was funny about the accent and not knowing whether people were asking or telling. I even told her about the woman saying she wanted to make love to me. Sam seemed to find that kind of sexy, like it was a compliment to her. I think she was a little surprised that other women found me alluring. We took a shower and headed out for a day of ass-kissing and new memories.

We didn't mention the wedding once as we walked around town. I thought about bringing it up, but knew it might be a sensitive discussion at that point. I felt off kilter a bit as if Sam had drifted from me. I hoped we would have an amazing day so she would loosen up and see that one night without her didn't change anything between us. I stopped and bought a pack of cigarettes, much to her dismay. I told her about how they seemed smoother than what we were used to smoking—she didn't believe me. She accused me of being caught up in the moment where everything was better. She said that the beer probably tasted better too, since she wasn't there. I finally convinced her to take a drag of the Marlboro and she agreed, they were a bit different. We made a vow that we both would only smoke in foreign cities. I was happy that at least one vow had been made in Holland.

We stumbled across a restaurant called Stingers. It kind of reminded us of an American Hooters, but there were some subtle differences. For example, we ordered a pitcher of beer and twenty wings. A few minutes later, a girl came out, climbed up on the table next to ours and did a little pole dance. We wondered what we would have gotten if we'd ordered forty wings. Sam started to loosen up a bit, it might have been the beer, or the half-naked women, but I think she realized that I was the same Dani I was on Thursday. By two o'clock things seemed to be back to normal. I worried about drinking too much because I was afraid of one of those stupid drunken fights we drama gals are so famous for. I couldn't stand the idea of a Saturday night of yelling about the events of Friday night, so I suggested that we stop drinking for a bit.

"Let's try some herbal ecstasy," Sam suggested as we passed a coffee shop.

"Are you serious? Have you tried it before?" I was nervous.

"It's harmless. Loosen up. I promise not to get you fucked up and try to kiss you in the moonlight."

I realized she was still a bit bitter and I needed to follow her whims. "Okay. Lead the way."

"Wait right here." She went into the coffee shop and came back out a few minutes later with a tiny bottle. "Let's go to that little pub that sits below the apartment. That way if you start freaking out, we can get you home."

"Or if I really start freaking out, I can jump in the canal and retrieve the key."

"And your panties. They're still floating." She laughed.

We took advantage of the slightly warmer weather and sat outside. The window to our apartment was directly above us, so I felt a sense of security. "Okay, madam, give me a…what do you call it? Give me a tab?"

"Just take the pill, Dani." She handed me the small tablet. "You don't have to try and be hip all the time."

I set the pill on my tongue and took a swig of beer. "Here's mud in your eye."

"God, you're a dork." She took her hit of herbal X.

We sat there for a few minutes waiting to feel the effects. Nothing happened. We thought maybe it was because we were trying too hard, like the watched pot that never boils. Sam went inside the bar to retrieve some more beer while I sat and stared up at our apartment. I wished for a moment that we could buy the place and stay forever. I was different in Amsterdam. I was less reserved, more at peace with myself. I thought about how I was wasting my life, my creativity, and my dreams by not doing anything at home. I thought about how wonderful it was to escape with Sam even though I missed our home and our families and friends. That's when I figured out what effect herbal ecstasy had on me…it made me think. Unlike pot or hash that just made me a little tired or goofy, X put thoughts into my head. By the time Sam came out of the bar, my mind was working a mile a minute.

I started talking before she even sat down. "We need to plan this wedding, dreamer."

"Holy shit. I was just thinking the same thing. Can you hear the canal? I can actually hear the water moving. I didn't notice that before. It's a subtle noise, but I can hear it. Where should we get married? Do you think everyone will come? What are you gonna wear?" She never stopped to take a breath.

I didn't answer any of her questions. "I kind of want to take a shower. I wonder if I'll be able to actually hear the shampoo bubbles in my hair."

"Suds." She giggled. "The bubbles are called suds."

"Suds." The sound of the word made me laugh. "Suds, suds, suds."

She was laughing so hard I thought she was going to fall out of her chair. "Suds." She shouted. "They're called suds, Doctor O'Connor!"

Then suddenly it wasn't funny anymore. We both abruptly stopped laughing and stared at each other. I leaned over and kissed her, right there on the canal next to a floating pair of underpants. She placed her hands on my face and kissed me harder than she had ever kissed me before. I put my hand on the back of her neck so she couldn't pull away. I have no idea how long we sat and kissed. The sky grew dark and the air grew cold, and still we kissed.

I finally got to take my shower, but the herbal stuff had worn off, so I didn't get to hear the hysterical suds, bubbles, whatever. Neither one of us had any desire to eat. I noticed we never really ate much when we traveled together. I suspected it was because we were both so afraid of food standards in other countries. Neither of us wanted to get food poisoning because we were shy about bodily functions. We knew it was mandatory to eat, that woman could not live on beer alone, so we each forced down a slice of pizza from a street vendor and crossed our fingers that the cheese was up to par.

The Red Light District of Amsterdam was packed that Saturday night; probably every Saturday night. It seemed as though every country was represented with its stereotypes. We saw Germans wearing leather and chains, Americans in their football jerseys and even some guys in kilts who might have been Scottish. The men were lined up outside any door that was lit up with a red light. We didn't notice an abundance of women.

We found a large pub on the corner of two main streets, so we stopped in and had a few beers while we got up the courage to go farther into the district. I remembered what Kyler, the hotel guy, had said about public restrooms, so I waited at the bar and got the key. I was cautious going in and realized that his advice was good. On my walk to the bathroom, I must have been touched at least twenty times. When I say touched, I really mean groped and when I say twenty, I really mean ten. Regardless, the men were very aggressive and I peed as fast as I could so we could leave.

We stood outside for a while debating where to go next. We had a ton of options and decided we would start small and work our way up. The first place we stopped looked like a mini-mall or a tiny movie theater. Following the illustrated directions, we went in, walked to a little booth, closed the door behind us, inserted two Euro into a slot and a curtain opened. We didn't know what to expect and about fell to the floor when the open curtain revealed a rotating floor with two people having sex atop a heart-shaped bed. We were both overwhelmed by a case of the nervous giggles. I don't know why we were uncomfortable with the situation; we were a happy, sexually active couple. It might have been because it was a man and a woman; it might have been because Americans are sheltered in our censored country. There was only one way for us to survive the ten minute sex show—humor.

Sam held up an invisible microphone. "Well, George, I see that Sven has really brought his A game tonight."

"That he has, Glen. And Inga is really on the ball as well." I giggled.

"It's a little-known fact that the couple has been practicing this event for years. It's really paid off. Look at their form, George. These two are totally in sync." Sam passed the invisible microphone to me.

"There's no doubt that these two are gonna go all the way in this event." I passed the invisible mike back to Sam who was in hysterics.

Finally she could talk again. "Oh, just look at Sven's attention to detail. He really knows how to play for the judges. He's smiling while he licks her nipple, that's a sign of a true professional."

"You're not kidding George—"

"I'm Glen. You're George," Sam whispered.

"Sorry, Glen. I don't know where my mind is. You're not kidding about his attention to detail. Every thrust of his pelvis is like a little dance. And let's not forget Inga's talent. She's taking it in the ass like a true champion."

"I've never seen such devotion in two so young. Wait, what's this? It seems as though they're changing formats in the middle of the performance here. Yes, it's a double flip and roll into a sixty-nine." Sam's face was bright red.

"Well, I don't know how sanitary that is, but they didn't seem to miss a beat." I was a little grossed out. "Tell me, Glen, how does one judge an event such as this?"

"There are three scoring categories, George. First and foremost, it's all about stamina. See how Sven is able to thrust in all positions, that takes some serious leg muscles. Secondly, it's important to consider attention to detail. Watch how Inga cups Sven's balls while they grind against her chin. Finally, we consid—" The curtain closed, our time was up. "Whew." Sam blushed. "I was running out of material."

"Okay, I don't know whether that was fascinating, disgusting or just flat-out awkward. I need a beer." I opened the door and let the next group of onlookers take our room. "Hey, the microphone is on the stool," I said as I closed the door.

Sam and I giggled as we headed to our next stop.

"I really don't know how we can top that." We were standing outside a building looking at the ladies in lingerie inhabiting the windows in seductive poses. "How do they determine which women take the first floor and which get the windows on the second?" I asked.

"I'm gonna take a shot in the dark, but it seems to me that the second floor beauties are a little sexier than those on the first floor. There's probably a price difference too. Notice how there is a line for the first floor babes, but the ladies on the second floor are actually picking and choosing?"

I looked around and realized she was right. "Yeah, they get

to be selective. Huh, I wonder who determines what floor you get to work on."

"You probably have to audition," Sam said and looked up. "Hey, that redhead on the end is motioning to us."

I looked up to the second floor then glanced around. Sam was right, she was pointing at us. "What should we do?" I wanted to run.

"Let's go up and see what she wants." Sam took my hand.

"No. I'm not going up there." I looked around and there were men laughing at me. "Fine." I followed Sam inside the building and up the stairs.

We entered a small, dim room at the end of the hall and the elusive woman from the window was seated on a velvet chaise smoking a joint. "Samantha, Dani, so good to see you."

I couldn't see her face, but I recognized the accent. "Hey. It's all good!" I remembered what her name meant, but couldn't remember her name. "Sam, you remember our friend from the plane." I walked farther into the room feeling surprisingly comfortable.

"Oh, yes. The banshee lady." Sam was as tickled as I.

"Alma. So what brings you ladies to the district tonight?" She passed me the joint.

I thought about saying no thanks, but looked to Sam first. She smiled and raised her eyebrow which I took as a sign of approval. I took the joint and sat next to our friend. "We're just out for an adventure."

"Well, you're in the right city and the right place. Is there anything I can do to make your adventure a little more exciting?" She placed her hand on my shoulder.

I thought about saying no thanks again, but looked to Sam first. She smiled and raised her eyebrow again, but she followed it up with, "Depends on what the excitement entails."

"It's all up to you." Alma extinguished the joint into a breast-shaped ashtray.

"Tell us someplace interesting to go have a few drinks. If we're feeling a little crazier later, we'll stop back by." I stood and walked toward Sam.

Alma thought for a second. "Try the Fruit and Nut Bar down

the street." She started laughing and blew us each a kiss.

Sam and I ran down the stairs arm in arm. "You weren't gonna go through with that proposition, were you?" I asked when we got back to the street.

"Hell no. There's no telling how many men she's been with tonight. She's an extremely beautiful woman, but I think I'll dance with the one who brung me." She squeezed my cheeks and kissed me on the lips.

I breathed a sigh of relief. "I love that we are so in sync on certain things."

"Yep, just like Inga and Sven."

We weren't sure what to expect from the Fruit and Nut Bar, but there was a line out front of the beautiful eighteenth century building, so we figured it must be pretty cool. When we got to the door, the bouncer asked us for fifty Euro each. I started to argue, but he informed us that the cover charge included the show as well as all we could drink. I paid the guy from my casino winnings and followed Sam to two seats at the back bar.

The instant we sat down, two friendly guys started talking to us. "I'm surprised they let ladies in unescorted," the taller guy said in a thick Irish accent.

"They didn't say anything about needing a man in our party," I responded. "Have you been here before?"

"Nah. My brother said it's a tourist trap, but we figger if it's all you can drink, then we might come out ahead," the second guy responded with the same Irish accent.

"I'm Pearse, this is Sean." The taller guy shook Sam's hand.

"I'm Sam, this is Dani."

"Dani, a little Irish descent?"

"Yes, I'm a real live O'Connor." I blushed.

"But you're Americans?" Pearse asked as the bar grew dark.

I started to answer but saw someone walking on the bar, so I grabbed my drink and nodded. The bar walker turned out to be a lean woman in her late forties wearing nothing more than what the good Lord gave her. She walked right up to Pearse and Sean and squatted down. Sean glanced at Sam and me like he was embarrassed. I felt bad for making him feel awkward, so I put my arm around Sam and kissed her neck. I think the guys got the hint that we were gay and I hoped that meant they would understand that we weren't uncomfortable around naked women. Sean winked and refocused his attention to the woman squatting in front of him.

She made small talk with the guys for a bit, and then smiled at us. After doing a little dance, she reached behind the bar and pulled out a basket of bananas. I felt Sam squeeze my arm, I knew she was about to die of laughter. I held back my giggles as the woman took a banana from the bunch and handed it to Sean. He held the banana for a few seconds and passed it to Pearse. I started getting the nervous giggles so I hid my face in Sam's shoulder. By the time I looked back up, the woman had the banana fully engorged in her vagina. She sat there crouched for a few seconds then started moving the banana in and out of her body. After a dozen thrusts, she removed the banana from her vagina and peeled it.

"If she eats that, I'm leaving," Sam screamed in my ear.

The woman held out the banana for Sean and he refused. Pearse held up his hand before she had a chance to offer it to him. "No, thank you though," he shouted over the music. She chatted with them for a few minutes more, then put the banana basket behind the bar and walked off.

"Wow, that was different." I finished my beer and reached for the next.

"So." Sean's face was practically purple from humiliation. "You girls are Americans?"

"Yes. We're from Dallas, Texas." Sam fanned his face, laughing.

"We're from Dublin." Pearse didn't look as embarrassed. "I can't believe that woman just fecked a banana."

"At least we know how the bar got its name," I said.

"Dallas is far from New York?" Pearse asked when the music quieted down.

"Yeah, several hours on a plane," Sam answered. "Have you been to New York?"

"Nah. I've never even talked to Americans before." He motioned the bartender for another round of beer. "Were you affected by September eleventh?"

It was such an unusual question; I didn't know what to say. The events of nine-eleven were years prior, not many people talked about it much anymore in social situations. Sam responded before I found any words. "It hurt, it was scary. I don't know that our citizens will ever feel completely safe ever again. It didn't affect us personally. Neither Dani nor I knew anyone killed in the attack, but we certainly mourned."

"It was tough to watch." Sean sounded apologetic.

"What was it like watching the events of that day from Dublin?" I didn't know what else to say.

"It was like finding out that your heroic big brother was in a fight and you are too little and too far away to do anything about it," Sean solemnly stated, again sounding apologetic.

"That's a wonderful analogy." I almost cried. "Thank you for that."

I could tell that Sam was touched as well because a tear rolled down her cheek.

"Hell, like they say in the movies...let's get pissed!" Pearse shouted. "No more tears tonight ladies. Bring on the banana show!" He touched Sam's hand and winked.

A few minutes later, another woman walked down the bar. This time she was a blonde in her thirties. She smiled at Sam and me, but went directly to our Irish friends. She chatted them up for a few minutes, then took a pen and postcard from behind the bar. She asked them something we couldn't decipher and they both pointed to us.

"They want to know your address so they can mail you a postcard," the woman said with a German accent.

"Really?" Sam looked at the boys and they nodded. She went on to give our address. I was surprised that she gave out the real one.

The lady wrote the address down on a bar napkin then reached for the postcard. She crouched up on the bar right in front of Pearse, and then she grabbed the pen. She sat there in a position like a baseball catcher, slid the postcard between her feet and we could predict what was coming next.

"Oh, my, Doc." Sam was turning red. "She's not gonna stick

the Bic in her—"

Then she did it. "Yup. She is. Damn!" The woman stuck the pen in her vagina and addressed the postcard by moving her hips in small, circular motions. When she finished she showed the boys then slid it down the bar to show us. We were amazed by the penmanship. She gave the postcard back to the Irishmen and strutted away.

"Do you still call it handwriting?" Pearse asked.

"Do you still call it penmanship?" Sam retorted.

"I'm almost afraid to see what's next." I finished my beer and reached for another. It's probably important to mention at this point that the beer glasses at most bars in Amsterdam are very small. In America, the average beer is probably sixteen ounces in a bar and costs three to four dollars. In Amsterdam, most places serve six or eight ounce glasses that cost only one and a half Euros or less. This is the reason we weren't falling over drunk; finishing a beer meant drinking half a beer or less.

A third woman came down the bar carrying an empty basket and a dildo. "That's it. We're out of here." Sam stood and grabbed my hand. "You boys have fun."

"You can't leave now. Aren't you curious?" Sean giggled.

"Sean, we've seen more tonight than our little minds can process. We have enough conversation fodder to last for years." I slid our two full beer glasses over to the boys.

"We were hoping to get a chance to talk to you more. We've never hung with Americans before, especially beautiful female ones." Pearse winked.

"You're such a sweet pair of boys." Sam kissed his cheek. "We'll be at the Dam Square tomorrow afternoon. Meet us in front of Madame Tussaud's at one and we'll buy you lunch."

"You got a deal." Sean shook our hands while Pearse returned Sam's kiss. "Please be careful getting home. Saturday night's crazy out there."

"You too. See you tomorrow." Sam took my hand and we made our way through the crowd of people as fast as we could.

"I can't believe you gave them our real address and offered to buy them lunch," I said as we walked toward the canal.

"Ever get a feeling about someone?" Sam thought for a

moment. "Something about Pearse really reminded me of you, Doc. Maybe it's the Irish heritage, maybe the smile, but I instantly felt connected to him. It was strange."

"Maybe it was the big brother remark." I sighed. "They were very sweet. Okay, so once again we've made new friends."

"Yes, and notice how I didn't kiss either one of them." She paused. "On the lips. See, you can make friends in Holland without kissing them with your tongue."

"Yes, I see. But next time we vacation, let's go to France. I'm pretty sure you can use the tongue there."

Chapter 8

We headed for the square at eleven so we could look around before meeting Pearse and Sean for lunch. The place was absolutely packed. Wall-to-wall people lined the center of the square surrounding a stage area.

I stood on my tiptoes and tried to see over the crowd. "Can you tell what's going on?"

"Well, Doc. I see a common theme among the signs. Most of them say something about olie, oorlog, or Bush."

"I'm guessing it's some protest?" I looked around to see the signs.

"Have you ever seen the name Bush on a sign where it wasn't a protest?" she asked. "Olie means oil. Oorlog means war. And we all know who Bush is. I'd say it's more of a peace rally than a protest though."

"Let's steer clear." I headed to the west side of the square and stood in front of some street performers dressed as robots and cartoon characters. "Here, take my picture with Gumby." I handed Sam the camera.

She snapped a picture. "You're not afraid are you, Dani? What's wrong with people standing up for what they believe in?"

"There's nothing at all wrong with a peaceful protest. In fact, I think it's beautiful. I just feel a little weird about being American in the middle of all this, like they're gonna assume we support the President or his war."

"I really doubt people make assumptions about anything

here." She took another picture of me, with SpongeBob this time. "Plus, do you think they're gonna beat us up, or make martyrs out of us because we're American? They're supporting peace here. I think that'd be a little ironic."

"I still don't feel the need to get in the middle of it, Sam." I put the camera back in my bag and caught up to her.

"You know, Doc, you really need to loosen up. Maybe becoming a part of something rather than a mere observer would be good for you."

"What's that supposed to mean?"

"It doesn't mean anything. I'm just saying maybe you should put yourself out there for something once in awhile. When you were teaching, you were very involved with student activities, student government and some of their causes. Ever since you retired, you haven't been actively involved with anything."

"I didn't retire. I took a leave of absence. Maybe I'm tired. I worked my ass off to get to where I was at the college." My feathers were ruffled.

"I'm tired of that excuse, Doc. Yeah, you worked your ass off and achieved a great level of success at a very young age. You were prestigious and you got tired. Wake up and smell the coffee, Doctor O'Connor. I'm an attorney now…at the same age you were when you headed the English department. I worked my ass off to get my degree too. I struggled and stressed to get where I am now. It has nothing to do with money, so don't lay that trip on me. So you got tired. You took a break. Maybe teaching became redundant for you, but you can't peak career-wise in your thirties, and then decide to just spend the next twenty years of your life sleeping while the rest of us continue our careers no matter how tired we are." She realized she was shouting and stopped. "Sorry."

"What do you want me to do, Sam? Go back to teaching and spend fifteen hours a week commuting? Go back to the same bullshit classes and departmental political problems?"

"At least you'd be a part of something. At least you'd have a purpose. Not for nothing, Dani, but I'm tired of seeing you wear the same shirt for three days. At least when you were writing you had a purpose. Even when you were painting and selling your art on eBay, you were contributing something to the world. It's hard to leave in the morning then come home eight hours later to find you in the same pajamas rummaging through the pantry." She crossed her arms. "You don't have to commute. SMU is right up the street, apply there. You have the qualifications. You won't be head of the department there, so you won't have to deal with office politics as much. If you think the classes are bullshit then maybe find new classes to teach. I don't know anyone who loves literature as much as you do. You had the opportunity to inspire others to love the English language. Christ, Dani, you made a difference all over the damn place. Now you rot away and live vicariously through everyone else's life. Get a clue, woman, because life is passing you by."

"Okay." I sighed.

"We talked the other day about having a wife and being a wife. As much as I like the idea of having a little woman at home to cook and clean, let's face it, neither one of us is cut out for the stereotype. We're too strong and independent. That's why we work well together. We have our strengths and our weaknesses. You're great with the house, I'm good with the repairs. We can find a nice balance and both take on the necessary roles to keep the household running."

I tried not to yell. "So you've been holding all this in? You're passing judgment on me every time you come home and find me lounging and eating bon-bons? How long have you been disappointed in me? How long have you wanted to tell me to get a life?"

"It's not like that, Doc. I'm not passing judgment on you. I just know you're better than that. I know you have a lot to contribute, but right now you aren't doing a damned thing."

"Contribute? You're the one who encouraged me to take a break, to write the book. You said you'd handle the finances. Fine, I'll deliver pizzas and pay the cable bill."

"I don't mean financial contributions. You know I'm not worried about the money aspect. I mean you need to contribute to society, to the world, to the community…something. Frankly, I'd be fine with your delivering pizzas if it meant you got out of the house and faced the real world beyond Lifetime Television movies. My God, do you realize you spent twenty minutes last month telling me about some show you watched on MTV? You talked about the characters like they were your friends. I considered having you committed." She leaned against a streetlight.

"I don't know what to say, Sam. I'm lost, I've been lost for a long time now. I have no idea what direction to take with my life. I want to write, I want to teach, I want to find something mindless and stare at a wall. How the hell am I supposed to know what to do? You dreamed your whole life of being a lawyer, if you failed at that, you had the hotel business to fall back on. I don't have anything beyond English to fall back on. If I don't teach or write, what the hell can I do with my life? I'm stuck."

"Find something that inspires you. Do volunteer work. Open a bookstore, a bar, a golf course, have a baby, I don't care, but find some freakin' direction and be active before you're fifty years old and wondering where the time went. You're scaring the shit out of me." She was practically in tears.

"Shh. Baby." I put my hand on her shoulder. "I'm sorry. I didn't know I was causing you this much emotional stress. I'll focus on finding something. I'll do something with my life, I promise. Please don't leave me." I started crying too.

"I'm not leaving you, Doc. I'll stand by you no matter what; I just want to see you happy. You haven't seemed happy to me in a long time and it's eating me up inside." She took my hand. "We're here to plan a wedding ceremony, and we're not leaving until we do it."

"I love you. I'm sorry, I didn't realize."

"I love you too. We need to go meet the Irishmen then we can start looking for a ceremony site. Okay?"

"Okay." I breathed a sigh of relief that I had a chance to make things right.

We found Pearse and Sean standing outside the wax museum a few minutes after one. They were looking a little ragged, but seemed happy to see us. It was amazing to me how Sam could go from fighting and crying one minute to being Miss Congeniality social goddess the next. "Hello, boys. So glad to see you survived the Fruit and Nut." She gave them both European-style kisses on both cheeks.

I followed up with some awkward half-hugs. "So, how was the rest of the show? Please tell me she didn't put the basket in any orifices."

"Well, she inserted something, but don't worry, it wasn't the basket." Sean laughed and took my hand. "We found a cool little restaurant around the corner. Does that sound okay?"

"Lead the way." Sam took Pearse's hand and the four of us marched around the corner through the crowds.

The charming, colorful restaurant was packed but we found a small table in front on the street. The waiter came out immediately to bring menus and take our drink order. "Do you serve Dutch pancakes?" Pearse asked and the waiter affirmed.

Sam, of course, found his terminology hysterical. "Okay, Dani. You're not the only crazy tourist in Amsterdam." Sean asked what was so funny, so Sam went on to tell them about the whole Dutch thing. They weren't amused, I think she made Pearse feel a little stupid.

The four of us sat in silence and watched the protest for a while before Sean finally broke the ice. "What brings you lasses to Holland?"

Sam looked at me like she wanted approval for sharing our quest. I smiled, so she explained, "We're here to plan our wedding ceremony."

"Yeah, I thought you were both into diddies by the way you acted last night." Sean laughed.

"Diddies?" Sam and I said in unison.

"Don't mind him, he's just twistin' hay. Diddies are breasts. We figgered you two were a couple when we saw you kiss," Pearse explained. "Can two lasses marry each other in the States?"

"No. It's more of a symbolic gesture than anything." Sam took my hand. "Maybe an excuse to have a big party and tell the world we're taken."

"So you're gonna tell the world in another country? This half of the world? Or are all your friends and family gonna fly to Holland to witness the grand occasion?"

"Not all of them, but a dozen or so." I flagged down the

waiter. "Can I get a Grolsch?" I decided I wanted to drink in case the Irishmen turned out to be annoying.

"I'll take a jar as well," Pearse said to the waiter then turned to me. "Don't worry, I'm not gonna get bolloxed, I just don't want a lady to drink alone."

Sean spoke up, "I'll take a jar, and one for the other lady, we have to celebrate."

"Thanks." Sam batted her eyelashes. "I'm hoping a jar is a pint."

"Yes. So why choose Holland and not some place in Dallas where everyone you know can enjoy the celebration?"

I looked at Sam and she raised her eyebrows. "I don't know. I guess it just seemed like a fun place to take everyone. At least here we won't have skeptics, or protestors or awkwardness."

"Nah. This is a pretty open-minded place." Pearse looked around. "Maybe if I can find a fella, I'll take a plunge in Amsterdam."

"Is fella slang for person with diddies?" Sam beat me to the question.

"Nah, a boyfriend. I want a fella." Pearse didn't bat an eye.

Sean laughed. "You thought because we were looking at gals with bananas that we were both after knobs. I had to get Pearse suckin' diesel to get him out there last night. I wanted to chase some brassers and didn't want to go alone."

"I think we may need a translator," I told Sam.

"Sean had to get me hammered to go to that place. You know hammered? Polluted? He wanted to get a prostitute."

"I see. How'd that work out for you?" Sam asked.

"Couldn't find one I liked."

"He shopped around enough. We were out until five before he threw in the towel. I think he was just letting on anyway, he's got a girl at home who would have killed him if he went to a brasser."

"My wife hasn't shagged me since she got up the pole and off the drink. I'm entitled, I'm just selective."

Pearse clarified, "His wife hasn't had sex with him since she got pregnant and quit drinking."

"You're expecting a baby? How wonderful." I patted Sean's

shoulder.

"Ain't expecting nothing anymore. She had the snapper six years ago and hasn't shagged me yet. Still love her though, can't help myself."

"Her name is Nora. She's a bit of a queer hawk, but she's a fine bit of stuff. I dated her a year before my brother married her. Thief!" Pearse threw a piece of bread at Sean.

"Okay, let me see how my translation skills are working for me." I sipped my beer. "You and Sean are brothers. You dated Nora for a year then you realized that you're gay, so Sean married her. She's a little weird, but attractive. Sean has a six-year-old child. You're young men. How old were you when you got married?"

"Thirty." Sean laughed. "Guess Irish whiskey keeps you young. I'm forty, and Pearse here is forty-three."

"We kept calling you boys." Sam laughed.

"I heard that and thought it was an American term, or else you were already fluthered." Pearse blew a kiss to Sam.

"Well, Sean, you're married. If you could do it all over again, would you have the ceremony here in Amsterdam?"

"Nah. I'd have it at home. That way I could drive by the place all the time and remember the day. It'd be a reminder of good times when things get bad. Plus we have a big family. I'd not wanna exclude someone who might feel hurt. Plus, what if Nora gave me a fifty?"

We looked at Pearse. "What if she stood him up."

"Yeah. If she didn't show then I'd be gee-eyed all alone in a foreign place. Better to be around friends and family for both good and bad, you know." His eyes twinkled as he spoke.

"You're a pretty sensitive guy for a brasser chaser." I hoped I had used the term correctly.

"I have my moments. I'm sensitive for a living," he bragged.

"Sean's a nurse. I'm a teacher," Pearse said.

"Really." I knew then why Sam felt Pearse and I had a lot in common. We were both gay teachers. "What do you teach?"

"English at the St. Patrick's College in Dublin."

"Of course you do." Sam gave me an I-told-you-so look.

"Do you like it?"

"We say our only prerequisite is a love of reading. I adore getting to be creative." Pearse started in on his second pint.

"Dani here used to head the English department at a college in Texas. She took a break to write a book."

"That right? I can't write for feck, but I love reading. Maybe I can read your book."

"Sure." I changed the subject away from my writing. "What kind of nursing do you do, Sean?"

"I work with the wee ones at a children's hospital."

"Who'd of thought we could be watching a woman feck a banana with a teacher and a nurse by our side." I smiled at the thought.

"Yeah, you probably took us for longshoremen. Young ones at that." Sean smiled back.

We sat at the outdoor table for hours eating Dutch pancakes, sharing stories and drinking jar after jar. When we realized dinnertime was approaching, we decided to change the venue. "Why don't we go out?" Sam proposed.

"Why don't we find a place for you two to get married?" Pearse replied with an evil grin.

"We have plenty of time to do that this week. Plus, a lot of places are closed now. When do you head back to Dublin?" I paid the check.

"We're here until Wednesday. I want to see the museums and Sean wants to hit the coffee shops at least once. We only came in yesterday for a mini holiday." Pearse handed me some cash for their portion.

"I think we should find the place for you to get married on Tuesday then if things are closed now," Sean submitted.

"I'm sure you two have better things to do on Tuesday than shop around for our venue," Sam argued. "We could have lunch again though."

"Do you have anything better to do on Tuesday, brother, than attend a wedding?" Sean asked.

Pearse followed his lead. "No, brother, I'm available for a wedding on Tuesday."

"We're not getting married on this trip, boys. We're just

shopping around. We'll probably bring everyone back in the summer or fall," I said, procrastinating again.

"Nah. You're getting married on Tuesday. You can bring everyone back and do it again, or you can have a huge party when you get home. But you're having a ceremony here on Tuesday. Sean can be best man and I'll be maid of honor." Pearse was serious.

"You're terribly cute, Pearse," I smirked. "We couldn't possibly have a ceremony in two days."

"Give me two reasons. We just talked for five hours, I know the story of your lives. You can't say you aren't sure about the wedding. You were made for each other." Pearse was counting on his fingers. "Don't say you can't afford two ceremonies. Sam owns a hotel, hell, have a reception there when you get home. You already have the rings. Don't say you want your families here. Your parents probably won't come, so you probably won't ask. Sam's family will show up, her mom will try to control the details and her brother will probably be too hung over to attend."

"Two reasons." I sighed and closed my eyes. "Because...well. Hell, Sam, you know two reasons, right?"

She stood beside me. "Yes. If we had the ceremony on Tuesday then we wouldn't have any procrastinating to do. We'd have to start our new life impulsively and take a walk on the wild side. Doc's too much of a fuddy-duddy to impulsively marry me in two days."

The three of them stared at me, awaiting my response. "Fine." I tried to think of an addendum, but nothing came to mind. "Fine, I'll marry you Tuesday."

"Don't sound so excited." Pearse grabbed me and lifted me over his shoulder. "Sean, take Sam to a coffee shop. I'm taking Dani to a nudie bar." He started to walk off with my struggling body. I could already feel anxiety and hoped it didn't show too much on my face.

"Pearse, stop. Tomorrow night will be the bachelor parties. Or is it bachelorettes? Tonight we all retreat to our rooms and come up with ideas. Set the lady down and say goodnight," Sean demanded.

Pearse lowered me back to the sidewalk. "Fine. I'll see you tomorrow." He held his head down like a punished child, while I reassembled myself, then he clapped and shouted in a shrill girly voice. "I'm so excited! I get to be a bridesmaid!"

Sam and I walked back to the apartment without saying a word. When we got to the bedroom she just stared at me as if she was waiting for me to break the silence. The look on her face made me nervous. "What?"

"You just committed us to getting married in less than forty-eight hours."

"I committed us? You're the one who used reverse psychology to get me to say yes. You practically dared me by calling me a fuddy-duddy." I sat on the edge of the bed. I felt a bit shaky.

"I was counting on your fuddy-duddiness to get us out of it. I wasn't daring you; I was reminding you that you're not impulsive, hoping you'd take the lead and keep procrastinating." She sat next to me.

"Maybe I don't want to procrastinate anymore. Maybe after listening to Sean I realized that it would be better to celebrate in the States."

"If you want to do it in the States, then why did you commit us to a ceremony on Tuesday?"

She laid her head on my shoulder. I wasn't sure if she was just placating me. I said, "Because I think I'd rather go ahead and elope now and have a big reception later. It might be easier for everyone, plus your mother won't take over the plans and insist on a church thing."

"Hell, Dani. She'd never allow our ceremony to take place in her precious church. That would be blasphemy." She laughed. "Do we have any hash left?"

"Gotta get fecked up to accept the fact that we're actually going through with this?"

"No. But when in Rome…"

"If we were in Rome we wouldn't have met the Pollard brothers." I laughed. "Then we could keep procrastinating."

"Maybe it was meant to be, Doc. Maybe we met your male counterpart for a reason." She thought for a moment. "It's amazing how much you two are alike."

"Yeah. Maybe he'll motivate me to chase my dreams. He's already talked me into chasing my woman." I reached for her, needing reassurance.

She pushed me away. "I think we should avoid all physical contact for two days, that way our wedding night will be special."

"Uh-huh, because we've never gone two days without sex before." I rolled my eyes.

"I know two days is no big deal, but we can at least show some decorum. We could even sleep in separate rooms." She stood up.

"You have your period, don't you?" I giggled.

"No. I don't have my period, jackass." She blushed. "I have gas."

Chapter 9

I gave Sam the bedroom and I took the sofa. One night of showing decorum and my neck was stiff already. I had a hard time falling to sleep because I started feeling bad about changing the venue knowing that Jack and Toby would be disappointed. We had replaced our own brothers with the Irish brothers.

I thought about calling home to tell Jack and Amelia the new plan, but I decided it was best to just elope and announce the news when we returned. I didn't want them to feel the need to hop a plane which would just give me added anxiety about Amelia's health and Jack's job. Sam agreed with me on this, it wouldn't be a true elopement if we told the whole world anyway.

I was surprised that Sam wasn't up and about yet. The clock read nine thirty and we had gone to bed early. I decided to sneak into the bedroom and grab some clothes. I tiptoed into the dark little room and bumped into a dresser. I froze and checked the bed. She didn't move—she wasn't there. "Sam?" I waited and didn't get a response so I switched on the lamp. "Sam, are you in here?"

"Yes. I'm under the bed." A soft voice came from below.

"What on earth are you doing under the bed?"

"I had weird dreams. I think I dreamed the building was under attack, so I must have crawled under here during the night."

"Maybe we read too much Anne Frank." I lifted the bedskirt and saw my mate curled up in the fetal position. "Come out, baby." I reached out my hand.

"I'm afraid to move. There's something sticky by my hand and I think it's a used condom. I'm afraid to move around for fear I might find something worse."

"I can't imagine what could be worse than a used condom." I gagged a little. "Just crawl out and run straight for the shower. We'll burn your jammies and pretend this never happened."

"Dani, I'm scared."

I couldn't help but laugh. "Sweetie, it's not like you can get pregnant from touching a used condom. I'm sure whatever's in it is long dead by now." I gagged again.

"No, I'm scared about getting married. What happens if we have to become all serious and grown-up?" She started to inch her way toward freedom.

"I don't think that'll happen. We're a couple of goofballs, and I personally have no intention of growing up any time soon."

"Can you promise me we'll still play video games and watch cartoons on Saturday mornings? Can we still have our Halloween parties and dash off to Vegas on a whim?"

"I can promise you all of that. I'll write it in my vows if it'll make you feel better." I helped her up. She started to sit on the bed. "Please don't sit. We don't know what your ass has touched."

It was her turn to gag. "And promise me that we will always be honest with one another. If it doesn't work, we will have the guts to call it quits and not stay in a marriage of mere contentment. I want happiness and nothing less."

"I promise to always be honest. We've been through a lot together, Sam. There's no doubt in my mind that we'll always be happy and one day be sharing a room at the old folks home."

"Well, you're older than I, but I'll visit you and bring you pudding."

"Tapioca?"

"Butterscotch," she promised.

"Better yet. You got a deal. Please go sterilize yourself."

By ten thirty we were both showered and almost dressed. I was flipping channels on the TV when I heard something hit the window. "Sam? Are you in here?" I shouted, thinking she'd sneaked downstairs and forgot her key.

"Yeah, I'm throwing away my pajamas." She answered from the bedroom. "Why?"

"Something hit the window, I thought it was you." I walked across the room and looked down by the canal. "It's Pearse Pollard throwing pellets." I was tickled to see him standing there in his argyle sweater vest and penny loafers. I opened the window. "Is that you, Romeo?"

"It is I, Juliet. I've come to sweep you off your feet." He dropped the next piece of ammo from his hand. "I've thrown stones at four windows trying to find you. Your neighbors hate me."

"I guess we'll have to move to a new neighborhood. Where's Sean?"

"He's banjaxed. We stayed at the boozer half the night. I figger he'll be up around noon."

"Do you wanna come up? It's gotta be freezing out there."

"Yeah. I don't have any socks. I forgot to pack 'em." He held up his foot.

"How funny. I forgot to pack underpants."

"There's a pair of drawers floating in the canal." He pointed. "Want me to grab 'em for ya?"

"Uh, no thanks. Come on up." I started to close the window.

"Nah, you lasses come down. I'm too hung over to climb all those stairs."

We met Pearse by the bakery and Sam gave him a pair of her favorite striped cashmere socks. "There's a parallel universe somewhere and you and Dani are married and half-dressed."

"Thanks." He sat on the curb and pulled off his shoes.

He had beautiful feet and I thought if there was a parallel universe, he probably would be my soul mate. "You have nice feet."

"Yeah, and they're as cold as ice lollies. Let's get a coffee and start walking." He put his shoes back on and Sam and I pulled him up. "Sean and I came up with a plan last night."

"I'm afraid to hear the agenda. How many pints did it take to come up with the perfect lesbian wedding?"

"It's a simple plan for two complicated women. Lemme run it by you, and you can either kiss me or give me a puck." He saw the look on our faces. "I mean you can kiss me or slap me."

We sat at a little table inside the bakery and the waitress brought three mugs of coffee. "Okay," Sam said. "Give us the details and we can negotiate."

"We think you should get married right here on the street surrounded by history. There can't be a building here that's as pretty on the inside as it is outside with the canals and cobblestone. We think it should just be the service performer and—"

Sam interrupted him. "I'm sorry, did you say circus performer?"

"Yes, we think a few contortionists and a lion tamer. Argh. I said service performer. Just him and the four of us, obviously you don't have anyone else here to invite."

Sam shot me an evil glance and I jumped to my own defense. "No. I'm not inviting the woman or her bicycle."

She laughed. "Are you asking me or telling me?"

"Funny." I rolled my eyes.

"We can find someone today, see if there's necessary paperwork, make arrangements, and by this time tomorrow you will be putting on your gowns and garters." He sipped his coffee.

Sam looked at Pearse for a moment then lightly slapped him. "I'm sorry, you said I could give you a puck. I couldn't resist. We don't have gowns or garters."

"Wear what you want. You can dress up for the party in the States. Did you plan it?" He playfully rubbed his cheek.

"No." I stared at my coffee cup.

"I gave it a lot of thought last night. Dani, will you indulge me?" She looked at me with puppy eyes.

"I told you when we got engaged that this was all yours to plan." I looked at Pearse. "She's a better planner than I. So, Sam you are welcome to take the reins on this one."

"I was thinking of having a huge reception at our hotel in

Dallas. I thought we could invite a few hundred of our friends and family, kind of what we did for Toby and Amelia when they eloped."

"You don't think they'll hate us for lack of originality?" I asked while playing with sugar packets.

"No, I think they'll understand." She smiled and squeezed my arm.

"And when did you think this event should take place?" I was starting to feel excited about all of it and actually felt a smile grow across my face.

"Well, I'm marrying an O'Connor and two Irishmen are planning the wedding as well as standing with us. It just makes sense to have it on St. Patrick's Day. Well, the day after since the seventeenth is a Thursday; we could do it Friday the eighteenth and have a bit of an Irish theme."

"That sounds like a great plan, that gives us six weeks to make arrangements." I kissed her hand.

"Of course I have one ultimatum or all bets are off." She sipped her coffee. "With an Irish theme, we need native Irishmen in attendance. I'd like Sean and Nora, and you and a fella to join us. We'd pick up all your expenses, of course," she added.

"I don't think I know a fella who'd fly across the world with me, but I'm in, I'm sure Nora and Sean would love to go." His face was glowing.

"Good, it's settled then. I'll call the hotel today and make sure the main ballroom is available on the eighteenth." Sam's mind was almost visibly working. "We can serve some Irish cuisine and Dutch pancakes."

"Irish food is revolting," Pearse noted.

"Dutch pancakes would be awkward with a formal setting," I added.

"Fine, we'll let the chefs at the hotel plan the menu, but I expect you two to come up with something to bring a taste of Ireland and Holland to the party." She sighed and then stared at the front door. "Oh my. Maybe he could be your date, Pearse."

Kyler, our gorgeous hotel friend, walked into the bakery with rosy cheeks and a crooked smile. "Good morning, ladies. How are you enjoying your apartment?"

"It's great Kyler. I think we might have misplaced one of the keys though." I tried to play coy.

"That's no problem. If you need another, come by the front desk. Any decisions about departure yet?" He pulled a chair up to our table and motioned to the waitress for a cup of coffee.

"Actually, we were going to stop by today and tell you we'd like to check out this week." Sam looked at me. "Thursday or Friday, Doc?"

It hadn't occurred to me that we would leave so soon after the wedding. I was hoping for a little honeymoon, but I knew we needed to get back to plan the reception. "Assuming we can get a flight, we can head out on Thursday, I guess." I faked a smile.

"I'll make a note. I see you've made a friend." He held out his hand. "I'm Kyler."

"Hello. I'm Pearse, grand to meet you." He returned the handshake.

"So, girls, why the early departure? I figured you'd stay a month." He pulled his hand back from Pearse's tight grip.

"We moved faster than expected." It was all I could think to say.

Pearse jumped in. "They came to plan their wedding. My bro and I talked them into getting married tomorrow, so they have to get back to the States to start the new life of wedded bliss." He gave me a look that said he hoped he hadn't revealed too much.

"You two are marrying two brothers?" Kyler asked.

"No." Sam giggled. "We're marrying each other."

"Ah. Another lesbian wedding. We get at least a dozen American couples a year coming here and tying the knot in our Dam Suite." Kyler smiled. "Where's the venue for your ceremony?"

"We haven't pinpointed it yet. We were thinking by a canal on the streets of your beautiful city," Pearse told him.

Kyler chuckled. "What is he? Your wedding planner?"

"Yes, wedding planner and maid of honor." I looked at Pearse hoping I hadn't said too much.

"Before you commit to a wedding in the cold streets, come see the Dam Suite. I think you'll agree that it's the most amazing room in the city." Kyler stood. "In fact, come right now. My friend Joseph is up there taking pictures for a brochure. He performs ceremonies and is trying to generate a little advertising campaign for the hotel and future knot-tie-ers."

"Do you think he would perform our ceremony?" I crossed my fingers.

"You don't have someone yet? This really is spontaneous. I know he will. He needs the cash. He's my best friend and just moved here from Germany. He's been crashing on my sofa, and I want him to find a place of his own. I think he charges two hundred. Is that okay?"

I looked at Sam, then said, "Sure." I knew she wouldn't argue. "Do we need to get some sort of papers in order?"

"Do legal documents really matter?" Kyler asked. "Nothing personal, but when you get home, it's pretty much about the gesture rather than the legalities, right?"

"Yes, but I'd like to have something in writing, just in case the heavens fall to earth one day and we are legally acceptable." Sam was annoyed. I recognized the tone.

"I'm sure he can get something in order before tomorrow," Kyler assured us.

We followed the beautiful man into the hotel, onto the elevator and up into a magnificent penthouse. In the back of the penthouse was a set of narrow winding stairs. We walked up single file and entered what appeared to be a rooftop atrium. The ceiling was completely covered with stained glass tulips, and the way the sunlight shot through the glass made the tulip images reflect onto the lightly colored hardwood floor. "This is amazing," I said, almost short of breath from the climb. The walls were a subtle peach color. Baskets of flowers lined a center walkway, and at the end of the path was a small covered terrace completely covered with various kinds of more fresh flowers. Windows surrounded the room, but there was no glass, they were completely open which let the cool air flow in, along with the sounds and smells from the city below.

"We'll take it." Sam took my hand. "I can't imagine a more beautiful setting."

"The hotel charges four hundred for use of the atrium, but that includes an overnight stay in the penthouse below. It also includes a room service breakfast. Anything else is obviously extra." Kyler turned to a man who was coming up the stairs. "Joseph, this is Dani and Sam. They'd like to have a service here tomorrow if you are available, they'd like you to perform."

He spoke with a thick German accent. "Another lesbian wedding? You must be rich Americans."

"Guilty." Sam held her head down.

"I charge one—" He glanced at Kyler. "I charge two hundred for the ceremony. If you have things to say then I'll do the basic questions and let you do the talking. Some people like traditional wording in Dutch, but most Americans just say what they have to say, allow me to bless their union, sign a few papers, take a few pictures and go on their married little way."

"Sounds perfect. We'll write our own vows, let you bless us and that'll be that," I said hoping it didn't come off as flippant, even though he did sound condescending.

"Okay. Now you go. I have to take pictures before the light moves. You want night or day tomorrow?"

I looked at Sam who shrugged. Pearse asked, "Which is more romantic?"

Kyler spoke up. "If you have a lot of people attending, then the day is better for the beauty of the room, plus it's warmer. If it's just you two and the brothers, I'd go for night time. The moonlight adds some sort of magic and tomorrow the moon is almost full."

"Eight o'clock?" I asked.

"Nine," Joseph said as he rushed us toward the stairs. "Dress warm. You don't want chattering teeth."

Kyler gave us a replacement key and went back to work while the three of us headed out to find outfits for the big night. All we had left to do was find clothes, write our vows and spend the rest of our lives in bliss. Simple enough.

Sean finally joined us looking a little worn out but in good spirits. They told us they had a plan for the next twenty-four hours, and we weren't given much room to argue. They'd decided that Sam was to pack her things and go off with Sean while Pearse would move into the apartment with me. They weren't going to allow us to see each other again until the wedding. I kind of liked the idea because I needed some time away from Sam so I could write my vows. She seemed delighted to go off with Sean because he wanted to grab some clothes quickly and spend the rest of the day and night at a coffee shop or a bar. I figured it meant for an interesting bachelor party for her, so I helped her pack her things, kissed her for a minute and sent her on her way.

It wasn't until an hour after she left that I realized that I had just sent my future wife off to spend the night with a perfect stranger in a crazy city. I felt better knowing that I had Pearse with me as a hostage until I got my Sam back. I told Pearse of my reservations and he assured me that he and his brother were harmless and delighted to be a part of something so exciting. I also explained to Pearse how I felt bad about taking up so much of their vacation time. I offered to pay for an extension on their holiday. He guaranteed me that a free trip to America was reward enough for the Amsterdam distraction.

I wasn't sure what I had in mind regarding clothes for the ceremony. I was a bit jealous of Pearse because when we got to the mall, he found the perfect gray suit at the first shop we walked into. We must have gone into five different stores before I finally sat down and cried from disappointment.

"Maybe you should tell me what you think you're after before you go off your nut." He stared at me. "Argh. What kind of clothes do you like? Tell me before you drive me and yourself crazy."

"I want a simple A-line dress." I wiped a tear off my cheek.

"A tank. That shouldn't be too hard to find. Stop looking so shook; we just need to locate a proper store. These are too casual. What color?"

I thought for a moment. White was unnecessary, red was too bold. "Black or navy? Does that seem appropriate?"

"Wait right here." He held up his index finger and then went into a store. A few minutes later, he returned smiling. "Okay, I told the lady in there what we were after. She drew me this little map that will get us to an antique store near Anne Frank Huis. What do you think of vintage?"

"I love the idea." I took the map from his hand and handed him his bags. "Did you remember to buy some socks?"

"I'm not a complete gobdaw. I got three pair of socks and I bought you some sexy lingerie."

"How do you know it will fit?"

He laughed. "I tried it on."

After an hour of walking, getting lost, drinking a few jars and walking some more, we finally found the antique store. We told the gray-haired, fashionably-dressed clerk what we were after and she led us to a small room in back. "You're the second today."

My heart sank because I knew exactly what she meant. "A beautiful American was in here earlier with an Irishman, right?"

"Ja. Do you know them? You'd have to, what would be the odds?" She laughed.

"We know them; they're shopping for the same occasion. Did she buy anything?"

"Ja, she did. She found a—"

"Wait." I interrupted her before I knew too much. "I'd rather not hear the details. Can you just make sure I don't buy something similar to hers?"

"That shouldn't be a problem. She bought a one-of-a-kind piece from my personal collection. I normally don't sell my own designs, but you know how money talks. She's a spender, that one."

"Yes she is. I'd rather have something classic and vintage. Black or navy blue. A tank dress, full length, formal." I made hand gestures while I explained.

"I think I have a few that you might like." She left the room.

"What are the odds, seriously? See, this is all meant to be, you both had the same mindset for the clothes and ended up in the same place." Pearse was awed.

"Maybe it's the only place around to buy something like that, perhaps someone at the mall sent her here too."

The lady came back into the room pushing a rack with eight or nine dresses hanging from it. "The other woman didn't even see these. She fell in love with the first one she saw, so I didn't bring these out."

"Yeah, she's impulsive like that," I said as I walked to the rack.

Pearse looked at a few then whispered something to the woman. The two of them left the room for a few minutes while I held dresses up in front of the mirror. When they returned, Pearse said, "Okay, I have an idea of what Sam bought. I wanted to make sure you would be a little similar. We wouldn't want her to be in a polka dot sundress while you are wearing a jeweled tiara." He pulled two dresses from the rack and set them aside. "These won't work, but any of the remaining would be perfect. The lady told me which one would be a perfect contrast, but I'm gonna let you choose the one you love. Personally, I think they're all juicy." He was starting to sound more and more like a woman.

I looked at the remaining dresses. "I like them all so much." I held up each one individually. "This one would be way too small. I doubt we could get it altered with the proper fabric in time. This one's taffeta, I think. I love the style, but can't wear taffeta to my wedding."

"Yes, that's more of a prom fabric." He took the dress and set it aside.

"I think this one's a little too blue. In the wrong light it might come off as more royal than navy." I handed him the dress. "So I'm down to these two." I looked at Pearse and he was grinning. "One of these is the one that's perfectly matched, isn't it?"

"Ja." He giggled.

"I'm leaning toward the one with the velvet straps, but I think I'll try them both on and take the one that fits better." I walked toward the dressing room. "No peeking."

"Are you wearing skivvies?" he asked and I ignored him.

Both dresses fit fine, but one of them seemed to have been made for me. It was conservative, yet a little sexy. I couldn't decide if it was midnight blue or black. The soft velvet straps centered perfectly on my shoulders and I knew with the right necklace, I would be delighted with the long A-line gown. "I think we have a winner, Pearse." I exited the dressing room in one flowing step.

"Oh, my." He put his hands to his cheeks. "I just want to cry, you're so beautiful."

"You're such a girl. Do you think we can find a necklace and shoes to match?"

"Right here." The sales clerk came into the little room with two necklaces. "I was hoping you'd pick that dress, so I pulled these from the display case already." She walked behind me and placed the first necklace around my neck.

"It's a little long, it kind of gets lost in the cleavage." I liked the silver chain and jeweled antique locket, but it just didn't make me sing.

She handed me the second necklace. "It's a velvet rope, so you can tie it to whatever length you like."

I tied the necklace and it hung perfectly on my chest. The velvet rope matched the dress and the pendant was an engraved white gold heart—probably a hundred years old. "Perfect. I'm afraid to ask the price of everything."

"You're not as extravagant as the other woman." She laughed. "The necklace is four hundred and the dress is seven. I'll have you know that the necklace was found in the street after World War Two. There's no telling what kind of history it has. The gown is from the fifties, probably custom made for a celebration, but I can't know for sure. I'll make you a deal and sell you both for a thousand Euro."

I turned to Pearse. "It seems awfully silly to spend that much money on things I will only wear for an hour and hardly anyone will see me."

"The other lady said the same thing. Her man told her to wear the dress again at the reception. She also said she was going barefoot for the service because she feared shoes would distract from the dress. I thought that was a little strange, but she's the big spender, I figured she was eccentric."

Pearse agreed with Sean. "Perfect, Dani. Wear the dress

again at the reception so your friends will see how beautiful you looked, plus you won't ever find another dress to top this one. Skip the shoes, maybe being barefoot together will be symbolic in some way."

"Did the other lady buy jewelry?" I wanted to know if she remembered to accessorize.

"She bought several pieces. She also bought a vintage tuxedo for the gentleman." She looked at Pearse.

"Oh, no. I'm gonna be underdressed, Dani. My gray suit won't fit in," he shrilled.

The sales clerk poked him in the shoulder. "I'm just kidding. They were going to the mall. I just thought I'd see if I could sell you some more." She laughed but Pearse and I were not amused.

We took the dress and other items back to the apartment. Pearse insisted that I go ahead and write my vows so that we could go out later. I didn't think it would take too long since I had a way with words and tended to be overly verbose. But I sat there for an hour staring at a blank page. Pearse had walked over to the Red Light District to scope out a place for our evening's festivities. By the time he returned an hour later, I still had a blank page.

"Okay, I'm all ears." He sat on the sofa and opened a beer. "Let me hear your sweet words of love."

I held up the blank paper and smiled. "Can I have a beer?"

"Depends. Will beer make you write, or make you forget that you can't seem to write?"

"Who knows?" I took the beer he handed me. "I know what I want to say, but I feel like it should start off with a bang."

"Just write down the things you want to say. Maybe things will fall into place and the perfect opener will come to you. You know very few people write the perfect draft the first time around. Jot down thoughts and we can tweak it all in the morning. Remember we have all day tomorrow as well."

He made a good point. "Okay, give me another hour then we can head out for our bachelorette party."

"I'm gonna have a kip then." He lay on the sofa. "Argh. I mean I'll take a nap."

I sat by the window and looked down to the canal. The image of Sam yelling up at me with a torn bag of panties popped into my head. I was reminded about how crazy she is; how she's never afraid to make a scene just to make me laugh. I thought about all the laughter we'd shared over the years. I thought about how it was because of Sam that I was able to come out to my parents. She gave me strength. I remembered when we went to Vegas and how Sam bet on number two over and over again until it finally hit, just because I told her to bet it once for me. She taught me about perseverance. I thought about the first night we kissed, how my body felt alive for the first time. Sam taught me about living. She brought life to my heart; she made me happier, healthier and free. Sam was beautiful and smart and funny. Sam was pure perfection in my eyes. I didn't deserve her, I thought. I then realized that if a woman like that wanted to marry me, then I'd better let her know how much I loved her. I was finally able to write my vows. It was just a few simple lines, but I knew I would have the next fifty years to tell her the rest. I wrote the lines just once and knew they wouldn't need revision. I finished the vows then stared down at the canal for an hour thinking of the times I had shared with Sam and fantasizing about the times to come.

"You finished?" Pearse sat next to me and stretched.

I snapped out of my daydream. "Yes. I don't want you to read it though. I want Sam to be the person who hears them first."

"Fair enough. You want to go to a nip bar or a gay bar tonight?" He was in good spirits.

"What's a nip bar?"

"Nudie ladies." He made a motion around his chest. "Diddies."

"I definitely don't want to go to another gay bar. I'm likely to get in trouble again. Let's hit a coffee shop and a bar and maybe go see some diddies later."

Pearse and I didn't get overly wild and crazy on my last unwed night. We had a nice dinner and talked a lot about teaching and books we've read. Next we went to a little pub and had a funny conversation about families and our childhoods. After that we hit a coffee shop and had an intriguing conversation about politics, religion and other hot topics. We finally did make it to a nip bar where we had an awkward conversation about sex, women, men and the big gay realization. We discovered that we really did have a lot in common and I was delighted to have someone with whom to share the eve of my wedding day. Around two a.m. we headed back to the apartment where I found a note attached to the door.

Dear Doc,

I hope you and Pearse had a wonderful night. Sean and I really hit it off, so we've decided he should leave his wife and marry me. Sorry to throw all this on you via note...but I felt you should know tonight before you took the time to write your vows. I'm leaving first thing in the morning to go back to Dublin with Sean. It's been a wonderful journey with you, and I'm sorry to end the journey like this. You will always hold a piece of my heart.

Love,
Sammy

I handed the note to Pearse while I dug in my pockets for the key. I didn't say a word, but he totally freaked out. "Bloody hell, Dani! They were supposed to be out having a craic, not falling in love. He must be gone in the head. I'm so sorry, I'll go find Sean and beat some sense into the gurrier." His hands were shaking and his face was beet red.

I decided to keep up the charade because I was drunk enough to enjoy Pearse's Irish temper tantrum. I wasn't sure how long I would let him stew; his mix of Irish slang and curse words were delightful entertainment. I knew the note was a joke because she always left me notes like that—notes that said she was leaving me for someone else. I panicked the first few times she did it, and then I finally caught on. If the note was a gag, she would sign it Sammy. She would never sign anything Sammy unless it was a joke, she hated being called that.

As we entered the apartment, I noticed another note stuck to the hallway mirror. I didn't walk over to it immediately;

instead I opened two beers, lit a cigarette, and sat on the sofa. Pearse had calmed down a bit and joined me on the sofa. "My poor baby." He put his arm around my shoulder. "You must be in shock."

"No." I tried not to smile. "I didn't really like her anyway. There's plenty of other fish in the sea. You and I really hit it off; maybe we should follow their lead. Hey, that would make Sam and me sisters-in-law! What do you think? Should we go to Ireland tomorrow and plan a double wedding?"

His face was white. "Dani, I...um...I don't know what to say."

I decided to stop the gag before the sweetheart agreed to marry me. "Hey, there's another note on the mirror." I pointed that direction. "Will you read it to me?" I did my best dramatic acting and put my face in my hands like I was fighting tears.

Pearse retrieved the note and read it to himself first. The color came back to his face as he wadded up the paper and threw it at me. I pulled it open and read:

Pearse, You fecking gowl!

She's not a slapper and I'm not thick.

See you tomorrow brother,

Love

Sean

"That's just not funny. You knew they were suckin' diesel, didn't you?" He forced a laugh.

"Yeah, sorry. I just couldn't resist. You're quite adorable there in your argyle vest shouting profanities at the top of your lungs. You probably woke the whole building."

"Are you telling me that your heart didn't sink for half a second?" He opened another beer.

I thought for a moment and had to admit there was a split second where my world was shattered. "Actually, yes. I did get weak in the knees until I saw that she signed it Sammy. That's always an indication she's kidding."

"You two are in for quite an adventure. I do believe you are perfectly suited." He smiled. "You lasses deserve each other."

"Thank you." I hugged him. "I'm going to bed. Big day tomorrow, you know."

"Goodnight future Mrs. Laine."

"Goodnight fecking gowl."

When I switched on the bedroom lamp, I found yet another note lying on the pillow.

Dearest Dani,

I'm not a lover of words, or a poet like you. (But I am a lover of the poet in you.) I have struggled over writing my vows and know that I will not be able to convey in words how very much I love you. Please forgive me tomorrow if I don't say exactly what should be said…just know that there is nothing more I want in this world than to be your wife…and I will be ecstatic and proud to call you my wife.

Yours, forever and a day,

Sam

I read the note three times then carefully folded it and put it in my luggage. I crawled into bed and lay my head gently on the same pillow where I found the note—knowing that Sam had touched the pillow a few hours earlier.

Chapter 10

My wedding day. My wedding day. That was the first thought that jumped into my head the second I awoke Tuesday morning. It seemed as foreign to me as the sounds of the street below. I didn't bother to look at the clock because I knew I had all day to do nothing but panic and get dressed. I lay in bed for what seemed like hours thinking about what I had gotten myself into. I had been married before, so marriage itself wasn't an untried idea for me. Of course, I was married to a man even though men were an unwanted concept to me. I stared at the ceiling and thought about the notion of marriage. I wondered what would be any different about our lives once we were married. We'd been living together for years, we had a routine, and we were monogamous. I tried to think of one thing that would be altered by this little ceremony. Nothing came to mind.

I rolled over and went back to sleep. I felt a little more refreshed and confident when I awoke the second time. I thought again about my earlier question: What would be different? Then it occurred to me that while nothing would be different, we would have told the world we're going to settle for that nothing together, forever. Maybe marriage wasn't about anything more than the ceremony. We'd still be together either way, but by having a ceremony we had the opportunity to celebrate our commitment with those around us.

Of course it was more than the ceremony, I knew that. There wouldn't be such a struggle in our community to fight for the right to marry if it was just about a party. Marriage was also about being legally recognized as human beings together in a relationship—two people who have legally agreed to conquer the world as one. Two people who took an oath to look out for one another, keep each other's best interests in mind and make decisions together regarding health, finances and family.

I thought about my twin sister and how wonderful it would have been to be able to tell her I married Sam. I remembered the day I went to the hospital and was forced to say good-bye to Amy. It occurred to me that if it had been Sam who was dying, I might not have even been allowed in the room. I might have been denied my good-bye. Marriage, for us anyway, wasn't going to change that. The ceremony wasn't going to be legally viable. There was a chance that we would never be counted as wife and wife. It was a chance I was willing to take in hopes that one day…the day that I am on my deathbed, Sam would be allowed to visit, and hold my hand and stroke my hair…and say good-bye when our journey was over.

There it was; I'd figured it out. Marriage is a promise that you won't die alone. Marriage is a way of saying I will take care of you when you need me to. I expect you to take care of me when I need you. Marriage is a vow that you will always stick around.

I guess I'd never paid much attention to the literalness of the for better or worse, richer or poorer, sickness and health part of the whole rite. But that was it, that's what we were committing to on that Tuesday, that was what would be forever altered. Our routine would be the same, but all in all, in the end, we would always be hand in hand. I finally felt at peace with what I had been procrastinating about for so long. I was finally ready to jump on board the happily ever after train and ride into the sunset. I was ready for the fairy tale ending, and beginning. I was annoying myself with all the Hollywood and literature clichés. I was giddy. I got out a pen and paper and rewrote my vows.

"You think you should get a haircut?" Pearse was playing with my unwashed, uncombed mop.

I ducked away from his grip and turned on the TV. "No. I think I'll wear it up anyway. I wouldn't want to get it cut, find out I went to a bad stylist and have a mullet for my wedding."

He laughed. "You wouldn't be the first lesbian who sported a mullet on her wedding day."

"True." I tried to think of a humorous retort but was distracted by the television. I was watching some sort of music channel and they were talking about Pink's song, "Dear Mr. President." "Man, I still cry every time I hear her sing that. She's awesome."

"Gotta love Pink." He stared at me for a minute. "I'm assuming you and Sam have a song. Do we need to go buy the CD so we can play it as you walk down the aisle?"

I froze. "Shit."

"Oh, God, please tell me you have a song. Who doesn't have a song? You can't just tiptoe down the aisle in silence. I guess Sean and I could play the kazoos."

"Of course we have a song." My mind was blank. "I just can't think of it." I started racking my brain. Finally something popped into my head. "Aha. 'Dancing in the Moonlight.'" I sighed. "No, wait. That was Amy's and my song. We couldn't play that or I'd be crying about my sister during the vows."

"What song jumps into your head when you think of Sam?"

"I don't know." I didn't know. "'Rock Me Gently?'"

"Maybe later. Right now we should think about music." He laughed. "You can't play 'Rock Me Gently,' it's a sexual connotation. You need something emotional. What concerts have you seen together? Maybe there was a song at a concert where she took your hand like the song reminded her of you?"

I tried to jar my memory. "Okay, we've seen Harry Connick, Nickleback, Stone Sour, Buck Cherry, Puddle of Mudd, Ozzie Osbourne, Alanis Morrisette, Sheryl Crow, Matchbox 20."

"I'm hearing blah, blah, blah, Ozzie Osbourne, blah, blah, blah. You Americans have crazy bands. Did she make a romantic gesture at any of those?"

"No." I tried to think of the other concerts we had attended. We went to concerts practically every month. "You know, she hasn't made a single romantic gesture at any concert we ever attended. Bitch."

"Let's not panic yet. How about 'Dear Mr. President?' It makes you cry, so it's emotional." He started pacing. "Yes, I want to think of our shitty president during the most important moment of our lives." I rolled my eyes. "Wait, I do know a song." I paused. "Well, don't leave me in suspense, wha—" "Shh. I'm trying to sing it in my head. It's by a new artist and the first time I heard it, I was with Sam. We heard it several times that same week and she commented on how it made her think of me. It made me think of her, so it's gotta be the perfect song." Pearse started to speak and I held up my index finger. "Every time I see your bubbly face, I get the tinglies..." I sang. "I've never heard that in my life." Pearse had me sing it three more times. "No, never heard it, and by the way, you should never sing again."

My mind jumped. "Colbie Caillat! We saw her in concert with the Goo Goo Dolls. The song's called 'Bubbly.'"

"Is it emotional and memorable? I mean it's got the word tinglies in it. Is that a word you want in your wedding song?" He looked and sounded overly concerned.

"It's a happy song about the feeling you get when you're in love. I think it's perfect, but sadly, I really doubt we're gonna find her CD around here. She's really fresh."

"Damn, for such a smart woman, you are terribly oblivious. Let's go ask Kyler where we can buy a little something called an iPod. We'll get some speakers too. Then we can find an Internet café and download the tingly tune."

"You just want an excuse to talk to Kyler," I teased.

"No. I just want an excuse for you to buy me an iPod." He was serious.

We went to the hotel and found Kyler surrounded by a group of female Swedish admirers. Between the language barrier and their obsession with his rosy cheeks, it took a good twenty minutes for him to sneak away. "Whatever you are here to ask, the answer is yes." He gave us both a hug.

I was halfway serious in my response. "Okay, Sam and I would like to you be a sperm donor." I tried not to laugh.

"I know, she told me that this morning." He smiled.

"Oh. Okay, that's just weird."

"I'm kidding. She came by this morning though. She wanted to know if there was a stereo in the suite. Then she wanted to know where she could buy some CDs."

"She beat us to the punch." I said in disappointment. "Although we were going to ask if there was a place around here where we could buy an iPod."

"Oh, I see you two are more technologically advanced than your counterparts. There is a stereo in the suite, and there's a place a few blocks from here to buy music. If you really prefer an iPod, you could borrow mine." He pulled a red Sony Nano from his pocket.

"That's nice of you, we appreciate that." Pearse took the Nano from Kyler. I could hear the disappointment in his voice.

"I was going to buy the iPod for Pearse as a wedding party gift. If we can't find one, then maybe we can borrow yours?"

"Sure." Kyler put the device back into his pocket. "I'll draw you a map. If you need to download some tunes, there's an Internet café down the block." He pointed north.

"Do you think we'll run into them?" I was hoping to see Sam.

Kyler looked at his watch. "I doubt it, they got a really early start. The stereo was just the tip of the iceberg. They gave me a list of questions about where to find things."

I was impressed that Sam was doing so much planning. "I am sorry we're being such a bother."

"It's no bother. I'm more than happy to help. I get tired of the same old where can I find American food and some aspirin type of questions. Do you want to know what all was on their list so you guys don't duplicate everything? Obviously she has the music under control."

I thought about it. I was still going to get some music just in case. Sam had slightly wild taste in bands, and I didn't want to spend the evening listening to heavy metal or ska. "No, beyond the music I can't think of much more we'll need. She probably has it all under control."

Kyler laughed and rolled his eyes. "She really knows her way around a hotel. She was barking orders at seven this morning like she owned the place. If I didn't know better, I'd say Miss Laine was the Miss Laine Hotel." He winked.

I dreaded asking the question. "Oh Lord, what did she order?"

"She had a list for the kitchen, a list of beverages, and a few requests for the room. She also already put in tomorrow's breakfast order."

It hadn't occurred to me to get appetizers or wine for the ceremony. That's why Sam was so good at running the hotel. "I hope she wasn't too much trouble." I sighed.

"Trouble? She's the best tipper I've ever met." He held up a wad of cash. "I'd be tempted to donate the sperm if I thought you were serious."

I tried to play it off. "Well, no need. We aren't even married yet. Children are a far-off plan at this point." I patted his shoulder and pushed Pearse toward the exit.

"One more thing, Dani." Kyler grabbed my shoulder and handed me an envelope. "She said you need to read and sign this before tonight. She had it faxed to us from some law office in the States."

I took the envelope, knowing what was in it. "Thanks." I reached into my pocket for some cash.

"No need to tip me. Your bride has everything covered." He patted his money-filled pocket and grinned.

Pearse and I walked out to the street and I did everything I could to remain calm. I started to open the envelope, but stopped. Next I started to rip it up, but didn't. "Do you have the map he gave us?"

Pearse handed me the directions to the music store. "Aren't you gonna open the note?"

"It's not a note. It's a prenuptial agreement. Part of me was expecting this, but the other part of me was hoping she would trust me enough to blow it off." My voice shook.

He stared at me for a moment, maybe trying to figure out what I was thinking. "Pardon me for asking, but if the marriage isn't legal in Texas, then what is the point of having a pre-nup?"

"Exactly," I sang, sounding a little like Ruth Buzzy. "I'm not after her millions. She knows that. I think this is more to appease her parents. If Sam and I broke up, they'd want to make sure the family fortune wasn't disputed in court by some angry lesbian." I could feel my blood pressure rising. I knew Sam did it because her father would have insisted. I was furious though that she'd thrown it on me that day of all days.

"I'm sorry, Dani. If it makes you feel better you could write an addendum at the bottom that says you get possession of the Pollard brothers and Kyler's sperm in the event of a break-up."

He was trying to make light of the situation, bless his heart for trying.

I looked at the way he was chewing his lip and realized that he was actually nervous. I think he feared that the pre-nup was going to ruin the plan. That's when it occurred to me that my Sam wouldn't throw it on me at the last minute if she thought it would be a bad thing.

"Knowing Sam, she wrote it herself and just had someone put it on her firm's letterhead. I doubt she consulted another attorney and made it a big ordeal." I tore open the envelope and inside was only one page—on her firm's letterhead as expected. It didn't contain a lot of legal terms or even a place for it to be notarized. It simply read:

I, Samantha Laine, do hereby acknowledge Danielle O'Connor as equal partner in all business and financial particulars. This document gives D. O'Connor right to half of all that I have during the course of our personal relationship. Should the personal relationship dissolve, D. O'Connor is entitled to part with fifty percent of all combined assets which include, but aren't limited to the following: the Dallas Laine Hotel, the Dallas bungalow, the Wyoming cabin, all vehicles, all artwork and the Deep Ellum restoration.

On the bottom was her signature and the date as well as a place for me to sign. I was awed by the simplicity and the trust of the document. She really was taking me into her life completely. But I was a little confused by the reference to the restoration.

"There's a Post-it note stuck to the back." Pearse pulled off the yellow square and handed it to me.

The Deep Ellum restoration is my wedding gift to you. I've purchased that dirty old factory in Dallas you told me about, now it's up to you to make something of it.

Love, Sam

I couldn't believe she remembered that Jack and I had looked at old buildings on my birthday. I realized it had only been just over a week earlier, but I didn't think she even paid attention. In such a short amount of time, she actually worked out the details and purchased one of my dream buildings. She hadn't just given me a building though. She had given me a vision—a purpose—a dream. I knew there was no gift in the world that I could give her that would be as meaningful. "Wow." I took Pearse's hand.

"So, what does it say? If you don't mind sharing."

I replied tearfully, "It says I'm a very lucky woman. I'm also a very wealthy woman now who needs to find Sam a wedding gift." I handed him the papers so he could read them. "Got a pen?"

He read over the words. "Damn, now I kind of wish she had run off with Sean." He looked at me. "I'm just kidding, Dani. Geesh. I'm very happy for you, you've found yourself a good woman."

"Indeed I did." I signed the paper and carefully put it in my coat pocket next to my heart. "Plus, she just sent the big ol' bite me message to her father and his family business. That's the best part of all."

"I guess you're her family now." Pearse smiled.

That was it. The question I had that morning had another answer. Why get married? To become each other's family. "Cool," I sang.

We walked around for several hours on a shopping mission. We found an iPod as well as various other things we didn't need, but had to have. Pearse and I were the proud new owners of matching Bull Dog T-shirts and Stingers hats. The best part of the spree was our jaunt into a bookstore. By the time we were done, we were both giddy from literature. We found old tattered copies of all the classics of the world—none of them had any value, but we both liked the idea of owning heavy bound books that had been read by strangers in a strange land. My favorite was a copy of James Joyce's *Dubliners*, as it would stand as a reminder of my new friends. Pearse's favorite was a collection of Dorothy Parker poems. I was jealous when he found it and tried to pry it from his fingers. He didn't budge. He said it reminded him of me.

We found the Internet café and downloaded thirty songs. It was fun choosing music with a guy like Pearse. He wasn't familiar with a lot of the things I listened to, and he kept pushing me to add some traditional Irish music. I told him "Danny Boy" wasn't really appropriate. He explained to me that Irish music consisted of more than just a few cliché pieces. We had some lunch and journeyed back to the hotel with our heavy book-laden bags. When we got to the top of the stairs we found a note for Pearse that said he needed to call Sean immediately at their hotel. Pearse ran inside to the phone in his melodramatic fashion—fearing there was some pre-wedding disaster.

"Everything okay?" I asked when he returned.

"Everything's fine. That was Sam. Sean is headed over here via bicycle and I'm taking the bike back to be with Sam for a bit. It's no emergency, it's just that Sean is no good at girlie stuff and Sam needs advice or assistance or something with a fashion ordeal. We'll do the switch back this evening since my clothes are here. I don't want to fall off the bike and lose the suit in the canal with those drawers." Something hit the window. "Wow, he's already here. I'll be back in a few hours. Have fun with Sean, tell him not to mumble." Pearse kissed me and bolted.

The strangeness of the situation struck me yet again. How on earth did we meet two Irishmen who were so sweet and generous? How on earth were we suddenly eloping instead of simply planning? When did we become such impulsive fast movers? We had been procrastinating for years, it all just seemed crazy like a bad lesbian novel. My mind drifted and I started plotting characters and names, thinking I would write the book.

Then Sean danced in the door. "Don't worry, lass. It's nothing brutal, Sam's just being a bit of a divil regarding wardrobe issues. As a man whose wife wears nothing more than slacks, I was useless. I guess gay boys are a woman's best friend on her wedding day. I, however, brought a six pack of Grolsch, so I get to be your second best friend." He held up the bottles and danced some more.

"I don't think I should drink until later. I don't want to pass out, or black out the ceremony." I batted my eyelashes.

"Oh, no. Dani girl, it's Irish tradition to be drunk on your wedding day. I couldn't find any whiskey, so Dutch beer will have to suffice." He handed me the green bottle. "At least one, for little ol' Sean who had put up with Samantha for two days."

I took the bottle. "Is she intolerable?"

"No. She's funny as shite and juicy enough to make me scarlet." He paused. "She's pretty, I mean. Although, we did have a little drama and stupidity at about four o'clock this morning."

I already feared the worst. "What happened?" I sipped the warm beer nervously.

"The phone rang at four. I figured it was probably you being lonely and missing your lass. I never figgered in a million years that it would be Nora calling the hotel. It was three in the morning in Dublin for feck's sake. So Samantha answered the phone, and it was Nora. I knew immediately who it was because I heard Irish shrill resonating through the earpiece of the phone."

"Oh boy. What did you do?"

"I grabbed the phone and yelled back. First I asked her why she was calling me so damned early."

"That was a mistake. You should have explained first." I knew how women are.

"Yeah, I know that now, thanks. Ass." He was starting to sound like Sam. "So anyway, Nora tells me that the pipes burst in the bathroom and that the downstairs was flooded. I asked her what the hell she expected me to do about it and told her to call me da."

"Oh, that sucks. Flood damage is a pain."

"Yeah, well me da's a plumber. Why she thinks it'll do any good to call a nurse…whatever. So she called me da and he goes over there and gets it all worked out. She calls me back two hours later pitchin' a bitch about the woman in my room."

"I'm amazed she could wait two hours. I hope she didn't tell your dad that you were cheating."

"I'm sure she did. So I explain to her how my Nellie panted brother was with you and the whole situation about you being gay lasses. She, of course, didn't believe a feckin' thing I said."

"So what did you do?"

"Sam got on the phone and tried to explain. Nora became irate and shouted every profanity she knew at Sam."

"I bet Sam laughed her ass off." I knew how she was.

"She did, but still I could tell she felt really bad. So finally, I said Nora could do one of two things. She could hop a flight to Amsterdam and see the wedding for herself, or she could stay put and get a trip to the States come March." He finished his beer.

"Is she coming here?" I was excited to meet the irate Irishwoman.

"Nah. Once I said we were getting a free vacation to the States, she shut up. After that she wouldn't have cared if I was sleeping with Sam, or if there were forty hookers and a sheep dog in the bed. She has dreamed her whole life of traveling and has never even left Dublin."

"Not to point out the obvious, Sean, but you're out of Dublin. Why didn't you bring her along?"

"Oh, Pearse paid for this trip. He was supposed to be coming with a fella, but the fella found another fella. So rather than canceling, he just brought me along. There were only two ticks for the flight."

"So did Pearse just have a breakup?" I felt bad for never asking if he was dating anyone, I just assumed he wasn't from his remarks.

"Nah. The fella was just a mate. He got a better offer to go to Greece with some more than mate fella, so he hung Pearse out to dry. Pearse didn't care, he likes me more than most fellas anyway."

"I can understand that. You're a pretty likeable fella." The word fella was starting to annoy me.

"I wasn't always so likeable, I'm afraid. When Pearse first told me he was a nancy pants, I acted all arseways and treated him like he was all blather and had a bad dose."

I tried my best to mentally translate. "Can you try speaking English for the next twelve hours?" I tried not to sound rude.

He thought for a moment before restating. "When me brother told me he was gay, I became a complete ass. I thought he was full of it and I treated him like he had a disease."

"Really?" I was surprised that someone who seemed so sweet could react so coarsely.

"I told him he needed to shag a good bird." He smiled. "Is that English enough for you?"

"I get what you're saying, but try talking like you're from across the pond." I was a little nervous about our impending conversation about homosexuality and was glad he'd thrown in some humor.

"He told me he had been with plenty of women. He said the lasses just didn't do it for him, but the lads made him feel complete. He reminded me that he had been with Nora and played on my heart. He said that if the woman who was the love of my life couldn't turn him, then no one could."

"That kind of makes sense. It sounds like Nora is a great lass." I tilted my bottle to indicate that I was trying.

"I still went on treating him like shite for months, maybe even years." He sipped his beer.

"You two are very close now. What turned it around?"

"We were sitting up at the hospital one evening after me da had a heart attack. He said that life was too short and that I couldn't go on hating him for being different."

I placed my hand on Sean's knee. "Did you hate him?"

"Stop flirting." He laughed, obviously uncomfortable with the conversation. "I didn't hate him. It's just that when you know someone your whole life and view him as your strong brother, you don't want to think of him being tender in another man's arms."

"I can see that. It would be weird for me to imagine my own brother in that situation." I thought about Jack and missed him.

"It's kind of different for you ladies. See, you are supposed to be tender. You aren't forced to be a tough protector who sticks up for your brother. I can imagine two women being affectionate. It seems sweet. Soft. Kind of heartfelt. I just didn't want my brother to be different."

I asked again. "So, what turned your feelings around?"

"That night at the hospital, I told him how I felt. How I didn't want my brother to be different. I wanted him to be the same as all the other blokes. He didn't say anything after I told him that. He just shook my hand and went to my father's side." He opened another beer. "Then a week later, he called and insisted that I go out to the pubs with him. I didn't want to go, but Nora forced me. She was tired of watching me mope around because I missed Pearse."

I reluctantly opened another beer while being enthralled by his story. "So you went."

"I did. He picked me up and we went pub crawling. We went to a sports bar and had some food and whiskey. Then he took me to a gay bar. We stayed for one drink and left. Then we went to two more bars and had various shots and beers at each stop." He looked like he was going to cry. "When the night was over, he took me back to my house. We talked in the car for a bit and he asked me if I noticed anything that the bars all had in common."

"Did you?"

"The only thing I could think of was that they all had people, drinks, music and food."

I thought about it like it was a brainteaser. "Seems like a logical answer."

"He said that was exactly right. Then he pointed something out. He said that although all the bars offered the same things, each bar was different. Different music played at each place. We ordered a different kind of drink at every place, and we talked to different people everywhere we went." Sean wiped a tear from his eye. "He said that if they were all the same, the night wouldn't have been any fun. If the same song played over and over again, if the bars only offered one drink, and the same type of crowd was at each place, then it would have been a boring night. He said what would be the point of having more than one bar if they were all identical. He explained how the world needs diversity to make life interesting. He said that one bar wasn't better than another—people go to certain bars because they like the combination of the differences at a particular spot. He said that people are like that—one's not better than another because they all aren't the same."

"That's a pretty neat way to explain it." I was impressed that Pearse went to so much trouble to make the point. Most gay people just blow off family members who shun them.

"It was. That's the night I learned there's nothing wrong with being different. It beats the hell out of idleness. And life has been a feck of a lot more fascinating ever since." He clinked his bottle against mine.

"So you're okay with him being gay?" I had to ask.

"I still cringe when I think of him sleeping next to a man. But I remind myself that he doesn't cringe when he thinks about my sleeping next to Nora. He's an amazing guy, my brother. As long as his Irish eyes are smiling, then mine are too."

I couldn't stop myself—I kissed him on the cheek. "You just gave me some thoughts. I think I need to rewrite my vows one last time." I handed him my beer. "Finish this for me. I don't want to be tipsy quite yet."

"Okay, you go write. I'll finish off this sixer and steal the rest of your hash." He smiled. "I need to be in party mode for tonight. I've never been to a lesbian wedding, I'm a little nervous about being best man."

"You'll do great." I dashed up the stairs to the little bedroom and got out another sheet of paper.

Chapter 11

After playing a few games of I Spy with Sean, I treated myself to an hour of reflection. He'd managed to turn the game into a little drinking adventure. We opened up the windows to the canal, and he said if he saw someone in a red hat, for example, then I would have to drink. He must have known there was a baseball team walking the streets because a steady stream of guys in red hats paraded by the window. I was smart enough to take small sips. I made it so he had to drink every time a blonde on a bicycle rode by. It was obviously bound to happen often in Holland, and his sips weren't as small. He was passed out within an hour. I sat on the sofa and watched him sleep. I thought about what his life must have been like, being a nurse working with children, yet having to put on such a macho front. I thought about the story he told me about Pearse and the diversity of the world.

I thought about how I was to be married in four hours and how that alone time on the sofa was my last chance to ponder the situation and bail if I wanted to. Of course I didn't want to, but it was fun to imagine the inconceivable scenario of hiking up my new dress, grabbing Kyler's hand and running through the cobblestone streets barefoot. It seemed like something out of a bad gay comedy where people can turn straight whenever they want. I thought about how the ceremony would impact my future. Sam and I would still live together—she would still fall asleep with her laptop and I would still get paint on the carpet. She would still work insane hours and I would continue to keep her dried-out chicken warm in the oven. She would still leave empty fast-food bags in her car and I would continue to clean out her car every Saturday. She would still get mustard stains on her shirts, and I would continue to pre-treat the stains before washing and ironing the shirts. It occurred to me that I was already playing the stereotypical wife role. It was a role I never thought I would be good at, but it seemed to be working. The thing was that I didn't want to be the stain cleaner and chicken cooker. I wanted to be the one with a schedule so busy that I had to eat fast food between meetings too. Was this ceremony going to clinch my position in the wife hall-of-fame?

Of course it wouldn't, I thought. That's why Sam had bought the building in Deep Ellum. Not only was she becoming my wife, and I hers; we were becoming business partners. She was giving me the opportunity to try something new, to have a place to go every day, to have something to get excited about beyond stains on carpet. I pondered my options regarding the building. I could turn it into anything I wanted; it was like a blank canvas or a blank ream of paper that just needed a story. Our future was just an untold story. I smiled at the idea and rewrote my vows one final time.

Shortly after I finished writing, I heard someone come in the apartment door. It was Pearse looking a little flustered and acting a little frazzled. "What happened to you?"

"Your girlfriend is impossible. I've never met someone so... organized." He paused trying to think of a better word.

"You mean anal." I knew exactly what he meant. I had a vision of Sam barking out last-minute orders and insisting that everything be precisely in its place, down to her perfect hair.

"Anal?" He didn't seem to get what I meant and blushed a bit.

"A perfectionist?" I tried to find a word that didn't sound vulgar.

"I would say Nazi, but that seems terribly un-PC in this neighborhood." He looked at his sleeping brother. "Think we can get him up so he can go get dressed and help the perfectionist with her frenzy?"

"If I pretend to be asleep can I just stay here and hide from future ridicule?" Sean spoke with his eyes still closed.

"Sorry brother. If we want a trip to the States, we have to see this thing through." Pearse reached out a hand to help Sean to his feet.

"Fine. But next time we work a lesbian wedding, I get the quiet girl and you get the one that barks." He stood and tucked in his shirt.

"I promise you she's all bark. She rarely bites." I didn't elaborate about how she does bite sometimes, but completely involuntarily.

Sean tried hard to stall, but Pearse managed to force him to leave by seven. We stood in the middle of the apartment and just stared at each other like we didn't know what to do first. Finally Pearse broke the silence, "Oh my God! I'm so excited I could dance." Then he broke into a bad Michael Flatley impression and I ran to the shower before he dragged me into the dance with him.

While in mid-rinse, I heard a man's voice from outside the curtain. "Doc, did you get Sam a gift?"

I was a little freaked out by the fact that I was naked and two feet from a man, and more freaked out by the fact that I had forgotten to come up with something for Sam to commemorate the day. I decided to act casual like it was no big deal because I didn't want him to make a dramatic thing out of it. "I decided to let her choose something. I can hardly compete with the gift she gave me. I'm sure she would much rather go find something together than have me impulsively get something just for the sake of a gesture."

"Are you trying to reassure me or yourself that she would want that?" He shouted over the sound of the running shower.

"Sam is not a woman who needs things. Trust me, she's never been one for want." I started shaving my legs and hoped Pearse wasn't going to peek behind the curtain. I pretty much had to contort my body in order to shave the back of my legs in such a small shower.

"Whatever you say. Hey, you could tell her tonight that you'll have a baby, then you could ask Kyler for a donation before you leave Holland." The fact that he sounded jealous made me laugh.

"I think I'd like to try being married for a bit before I commit myself to motherhood. Besides, it's not Kyler's genes I'm after anymore."

"Oh really?" He sounded like he was ecstatic and trying to remain casual. "Whose genes are you after?"

"I think an O'Connor-Pollard baby would be ideal, Pearse." It felt weird to say it out loud given that we had only met a few days earlier. You just know these things sometimes, I guess.

"I don't know, Doc. That's a lot of Irish. Aren't you worried that he'd be a whiskey-drinking, potato-eating redhead?"

I wasn't in the mood to start planning a family and debating genetics an hour before my wedding. "How about we work out the details of that down the road? Right now I'd like a little privacy so I can get out of here before the prune fingers set in."

He pulled the curtain open and stuck his head in and looked me up and down. "Honey, prune fingers are the least of your worries. You have to wedge your forty-year-old breasts in a fifty-year-old dress."

"I'm not forty," I said as I pushed his head back through the curtain. "Why don't you go get dressed."

Suddenly the curtain ripped open and a naked Irishman stepped into the shower. "Why don't you go get dressed? I have to shower." He stood proudly in front of me like he was giving me a view of his anatomy for future genetic debate. "That's right, take a long look. Loooong." Then he giggled and covered himself.

I was totally embarrassed and found myself trying not to giggle. I couldn't believe I had just stood in the shower with a naked man. I guess I could say that I'd done it all in the final days leading up to our ceremony. I wondered if Sam was staring down a naked Sean at that moment. I hoped not, but chuckled at the idea. I exited the shower, dried myself off and dashed up to the bedroom to begin the process of getting girly. I always enjoyed getting dressed up, especially for occasions with Sam. She was constantly able to outdo me, yet always completely complimentary in return.

Half an hour later, my hair was dried and styled. My makeup

was applied with great care under the leadership of Pearse Pollard. Who knew there was a way to make my eyelashes look longer? My jewelry was in place, with the velvet necklace tied to the perfect length, in a double knot of course. Finally it was time to don the dress. I pulled it over my head, careful not to mess my coif. I fixed the straps to settle them centered on my shoulders, then backed up to Pearse for the zipper. "It won't go up, Doc." The seriousness in his voice told me he wasn't messing around for once.

"That's not possible. It's not like I gained ten pounds in two days. Try it again." My heart started beating faster.

I felt him pull the bottom of the dress with one hand and tug upward on the zipper with the other. The next sound I heard was that of a fifty-year-old dress splitting across the back. "Oh, feck! I've done it now!" His voice was shrill like a woman who'd just seen a mouse.

"Please tell me the dress didn't rip. Tell me that was the sound of the zipper going to the top," I begged.

"Sorry, dear. The zipper was sticky and I tugged too hard. It's not a big tear, but we need to close it so we can get the zipper up." He sounded apologetic even though it wasn't his fault.

I racked my brain to think of something that could hold the tear closed for a few hours. "There's a safety pin we've been using for the hash. Will that work?"

"No, that would only close the gap a little. I think I can sew it. I can go to the hotel and ask for a sewing kit." He sighed.

I looked at the digital clock. "We don't have time for a home economics experiment. We need to leave here in ten minutes." I tried to remain calm.

"We could just head to the hotel and fix it when we get there."

"It's bad enough that I'm walking the streets barefoot. I'm not going out with my dress half zipped and my bra hanging out." I sounded like such a woman.

"Remain calm. I have an idea." Two seconds later he was out the door and barreling down the stairs.

I touched up my makeup and fidgeted with my hair. Two minutes later, Pearse dashed back into the room. "Please tell me you found something."

"I did. I got a roll of duct tape from a guy who lives downstairs. I noticed earlier that he had placed duct tape over the number on his door. I thought it was a little odd so it stuck in my head. Thank goodness he was home."

"Pearse you can't fix a dress with tape." It seemed a little tacky—pardon the pun.

"We have limited options. Plus now you have something borrowed." He grinned. "You know—something old, something new, something borrowed, something blue."

"Does that mean we have to give it back?" I thought about having to remove the tape from the dress and track down the neighbor before we left for the airport.

"I think we can just return the rest of the roll. I doubt he'd want the three-inch strip back. Look at it this way, if you ever write about the experience, you can title it How I Wore Duct Tape to My Wedding."

I laughed and relaxed. "That's not a bad idea, although there have been many strange things about this trip. That is a better title than Why My Panties Are Floating in the Canal."

"Even better than Why Is There a Naked Irishman in My Shower?"

I flashed back to the image and shuddered. "Let's never speak of that again. So what's my something old, new and blue?"

"The jewelry is old, the dress is blue." He thought for a moment. "And your friends are new."

"You feel like an old friend to me." I heard the zipper go up. "So we're set? Can you see the tape?"

"We're all set. No tape in sight." He turned me toward the mirror. "And you, my dear old friend, are beautiful."

I looked in the mirror and saw how I was going to look in Sam's eyes. I hoped it was good enough. It was the first time I felt really nervous and was glad that there wouldn't be a large crowd of people waiting in the room. Of course, I did have a secret fantasy that everyone had flown out to surprise us. I wouldn't have put it past Sam to arrange that. The image of all our friends and family danced into my head and I drifted into a scenario of how I should react.

"Hello." Pearse snapped his fingers. "We gotta go, Doc. It's time to face your destiny."

I flashed back to reality and followed him down the stairs. "I should have worn shoes, my feet are going to be filthy from walking."

When he opened the door, I was face to face with a white horse attached to a flowery carriage. "Then we'll let someone else do the walking." He took my hand and guided me to the seat. "I'll see you at the hotel."

"You're not riding with me?" I scooted to the side to make room for my friend.

"I'm not allowed. It was important to Sam that you got a quick tour of the city via carriage." He handed me a blanket for my lap, kissed my hand and headed down the street.

I knew what it was all about. She didn't want my bicycle tour with a stranger to be my favorite memory of the Amsterdam streets. She had to give me one last hurrah, in style—in Samantha Laine style. I was tickled, and I smiled throughout the entire ride, past every building, around every corner, and despite every road bump. The longer I rode, the more the anticipation built. I was so anxious to get to see Sam that I practically jumped out of the carriage before it stopped in front of the hotel. Pearse and Kyler waited out front for my arrival.

"And you didn't even muss your hair." Pearse said as he took my arm and escorted me through the glass doors.

"You look beautiful." Kyler kissed my cheek and whispered prost in my ear. I was pretty sure it meant something like good health, but I didn't want to ruin the moment by asking, so I returned the kiss, thanked him and followed Pearse into the elevator.

"Are you nervous?" Surprisingly, I was the one who asked.

"Oh, my belly is all full of butterflies. I can't believe this is happening. I'm so excited I could scream." He smiled, then probably realized he was acting silly. "Are you okay? Do you need anything?"

"I'm nervous, but I'll feel better once I see Sam." I took a deep breath as the elevator doors opened. I expected to see her on the other side of the doors and was a little disappointed.

"She's waiting upstairs. It takes a while to get a woman in a dress through the narrow staircase."

"She's really there, right? She didn't run off with Sean and leave me a note? I'd rather not climb the stairs if I don't have to." Part of me was joking, and part of me wanted to vomit at the thought.

"She's really there. Listen." He pointed toward the ceiling.

I closed my eyes to concentrate and heard the sound of violins playing from the rooftop. "That woman thinks of everything." We slowly climbed the stairs to our final destination.

At the top, Pearse stood in front of me and took both my hands in his and said, "May your days be many and your troubles be few. May all God's blessings descend upon you. May peace be within you, may your heart be strong. May you find what you're seeking wherever you roam." He then stepped to my side and allowed me to see what was ahead.

The rooftop was lit by candlelight. Hundreds of flowers created an aisle leading to a candlelit altar. "Oh my." I couldn't find the words, so I just repeated, "Oh my." Beneath the altar stood Sam, surrounded by flowers and bathed in candlelight. Her blonde hair was curled into small ringlets and her eyes looked so blue above her burgundy velvet dress. She wore a diamond necklace that I had never seen, obviously an antique that hang perfectly between her strong collarbones.

"She's beautiful." The violinists started playing again, and it took me a minute to recognize the song. "At Last."

"At last, indeed." Pearse locked his arm around my own and slowly walked me to Sam. When I was standing in the proper place next to my future wife, he took his own place behind us next to his brother.

Joseph, the ordained German, stood before us in a black cloak and white gloves. "Good evening ladies. I trust you are both here happily, and willingly with love in your hearts and peace in your mind."

"Yes," we said in unison as Sam took my hand.

"Good, then we will move on so you can begin your extraordinary life together—plus it's kind of cold to be standing barefoot on a rooftop." He motioned toward our feet.

The cold air didn't affect me until he mentioned it, then my teeth started to chatter a bit. I felt Sam squeeze my hand and that seemed to warm me.

"Have you written vows, or shall I just say something traditional?"

"Both," Sam whispered and pulled a sheet of paper from her cleavage.

I panicked. I had left my vows on the dresser at the apartment!

"Okay, Miss Laine, why don't you begin," Joseph whispered back. "But you'll have to speak up so everyone can hear you."

I almost laughed because I thought he was making a joke about the small party of two behind us. As Sam and I turned to face each other, I noticed the presence of one more person out of the corner of my eye. I sensed who it was and didn't acknowledge him for fear it might spoil the romance. Sam's brother, Tobias, always had a way of making me laugh at inappropriate times.

Sam's hands shook as she unfolded the wrinkled piece of yellow paper. "I don't know whether I'm nervous or cold." She laughed and winked. "Okay." She took a deep breath and began. "Dani, I love the way you squint when you read, but refuse to wear your glasses. I love the way you do a happy dance when you think no one is looking. I love the way you cry when you watch fireworks and talk about the vibrant colors. I love the way you're good to me, even when I'm grumpy. I love the way you smile when you walk in the door, and I love that I can't help but to smile too. I love the way you light up a room—the way you light up the world. I love the way you care about our home and the way you make me feel at home. I love the way you are my home. Today we become family. I vow to always be here for you, next to you, no matter what. I promise to love you unconditionally today and always."

I felt like I should say something, but the lump in my throat kept me frozen. It took me a minute to settle and let the tears fall before I could touch her hand. The words resonated in my head and were absorbed in my heart. "Thank you." It was all I could get out.

Joseph whispered, "Your turn, Miss O'Connor."

I shot a panicked sideways glance toward Pearse hoping he would know what I had forgotten. He must have because he tapped the side of his head and winked. He knew as well as I did that after rewriting my vows so many times I had to have memorized them. I wasn't sure I could recite them perfectly, but I did my best to improvise. I took a deep breath and let the cold air fill my lungs before I took Sam's hands into my own.

"I stand here awed
On a cold Holland night
The fact that you're here
Means I got something right.
I stand here smitten
And unable to breathe
Knowing we're bound
And unable to leave
I stand here smiling
And promise you this
I've loved you all along
From our first nervous kiss
And I'll love you forever
Till my last breath of air
I'll love you despite
Where you tossed my underwear
I'll love you every second
Of every single day
And I'll love you kindly
In every single way
I'll love you sweetly
Even when you're cruel
I'll love you passionately
For I'm a besotted fool
I'll love you like family
Unconditionally true
And from this moment on
I pledge my soul to you
I offer you my hand
To walk the world as one
I offer you my smile

And a lifetime of fun
I offer you my shoulder
When you need a place to hide
I'll be your best friend,
And remain by your side."

We stood there in silence for a moment just staring into each other's eyes, both of us obviously unable to speak and fighting the urge to cry. We slowly turned ourselves back to Joseph who continued the ceremony. His teeth were chattering. "Do you Samantha Laine promise to love and cherish Dani in sickness and health, good times and bad, today and always?"

"I promise." Her voice squeaked.

"Do you Danielle O'Connor promise the same? To love and cherish Samantha in sickness and in health, in good times and bad, today and always?"

"I promise."

"Are there rings present?" Joseph looked to the men.

"Got 'em right here." Toby stood next to us with our rings in his open hands. He looked tired, but handsome as usual with his wavy hair and dancing blue eyes. I was glad to see he actually had donned a tie for the occasion, although it didn't match his blue suit and red vest. "Samantha, please take the ring and place it on Danielle's finger." Joseph waited until Sam did as she was told. "Now repeat after me. I give you this ring as a symbol of my eternal love and devotion."

"I give you this ring, Dani, as a symbol of my eternal love and devotion."

"Danielle, please follow suit." Joseph was obviously freezing.

"I give you this ring, Sam, as a symbol of my eternal love and devotion." I noticed how cold her hands were and was anxious to warm them in my own.

"By the power vested in me by the online Church of Life, I am pleased to pronounce you wife, and well—wife." He tried his best to be poetic. "You may kiss."

The violins started playing Pachelbel's *Canon in D*—very beautiful and surprisingly traditional. It was perfect.

Sam leaned in and placed her lips against mine. It was a slow, soft gentle kiss upon a candlelit rooftop on a cold Holland night.

It was the sweetest moment of my life. I was warm and giddy with excitement, yet I had a sense of peace I had never felt before.

Chapter 12

Our kiss was broken by the sound of three men clapping. The two Irish brothers shouted "Slainte!" while the American brother shouted "It's about time!" He always had a way with words.

We thanked Joseph who felt the need to kiss us both on the lips. Next we were met with hugs and kisses from the men behind us. When Sam started relaying the story to Pearse about how nervous she was, Toby pulled me aside.

"I need to talk to you before we go celebrate." His voice sounded serious.

"I'm so glad you're here." I hugged him again. "Is everything okay? Amelia?"

"Everyone's fine. I'm glad to be here. I was already in France, so this was no great feat." Even though he looked fantastic with his new buzz haircut, blue suit and striped tie, he looked a little gray in the face.

"What do we need to talk about?" My stomach started feeling jittery.

"This is a talk I have waited thirty years to have with the person who married my sister. Even though I already love you like a sister, and trust you with my own life, I would be remiss if I didn't say what I have been waiting to say for so long."

"Ah." I knew what was coming—the be good to her speech. "Go ahead, big brother. Show me what a tough guy you are."

"Don't make me laugh, Doc. This is very serious." He fought a smile. "Don't let her work so many hours that she neglects you. Don't let her be oblivious to your needs. When she gets that attitude of indifference, just smack her on the head and tell her to wake up."

I couldn't help but burst out laughing. "Are you serious? What about the be good to my sister and if you ever hurt her, I'll kill you speech?"

"I already gave her that speech earlier. She promised to never hurt you." He smiled. "I know what the members of the Laine family are like, Doc. We're an evil breed who are work-driven and often forget our priorities. Look at me for example. I'm off working in France while my pregnant wife is shacking up with your brother."

"You really should go be with her, Toby."

"I know, I'm flying back with you two on Thursday." He hugged me again. "Welcome to the family officially. I've wanted this day to come since the first night we played pool at Splinter's."

"Me too." I sighed. "No, I think I've wanted this day my whole life. Now let me go find my wife." I liked the way that sounded even though it seemed so foreign.

Before walking over to join Sam and the others, I stopped to admire her for a moment. I liked watching her and the way she spoke to the others. She seemed genuinely interested in what they had to say. That's what I always loved about Sam—the way she made others feel so comfortable and confident. Her best feature—a new feature—was the diamond ring on her hand. The way the candles reflected the little diamonds made her hand seem so fragile in comparison to their strength. I couldn't wait to hold that hand for the rest of my life. I practically ran to her side.

"Hello wife." I grinned from ear to ear.

"Hello, little missus." She took my hand and looked at my ring. "This looks perfect on your dainty little fingers."

"I know! The ring alone was worth all the butterflies." I couldn't stop smiling.

"I think we should venture down the stairs and let the violinists leave before they freeze their necks off." Sean pulled us both toward the stairs. "I have to admit, I've never seen such beauties. It's enough to make me wish I was a lesbian." He winked at Pearse.

We followed the four men to the deliciously warm penthouse below and were greeted by two men and a woman in tuxedos holding champagne glasses. They passed off the glasses to the six of us and went to the kitchen, returning a few minutes later with serving trays loaded with trendy little appetizers to suit every palate. Joseph left the room and when he returned a minute later, soft music started playing from faraway speakers. "I will leave you to your celebrating, but before I do I'd like to make a toast to the happy couple." He lifted his champagne glass for half a second, tossed the contents down his throat and was out the door before any of us had a chance to partake in the toast.

"Geez, Sam. Forget to tip him or something?" I asked.

"No, I might have tipped him too well. He's probably heading to the District for some action."

Pearse stepped in. "That's the problem with online ministers. They're always running off to hookers. You don't have that problem in the Catholic Church. Those guys know the altar boys will wait up for them."

Sam, Toby and I stared at Pearse and didn't crack a smile. Sean realized that his brother must have offended us. "I'm sorry. One glass of champagne and he can't be proper in polite company."

Finally the three of us laughed hysterically. "Sorry, Pearse. It's a game we've played for years—make strangers feel awkward when they make religious jokes. We've done it so long it's practically involuntary. That was really very funny." He smacked Pearse on the back.

"Really? If I've offended you I can leave." He was red-faced.

"Honestly. You're in on the joke, so now you're one of us," Sam reassured him.

"That's right. Welcome to the screwed up, agnostic bunch of Laine kids." It felt good to include myself as a Laine, and Sam smiled when I said it.

The five of us lounged around the beautiful penthouse for hours telling tales of our childhoods while the visitors in tuxedos brought us trays and trays of foods and drinks from all over the world. I couldn't have asked for a more perfect evening. I only wished that my own siblings could have been there. I was envious of the other four for having relatives present and I would have given my own heart to have had my sister, Amy, sitting next to me. I wished I could have called Jack, but I knew it would be easier if I just waited and shared it all with him when I returned. It wasn't a night for missing loved ones. It was a night for appreciating my new family.

Throughout the evening, Sam had given me little flashes of what she was wearing underneath her long gown. I could only assume she'd done her shopping at the Red Light District. Each time she knew none of the guys was looking her way; she would pull up her gown and show me her black lace garters, or pull down the front of her dress to show the matching corset. By the time we finished our third tray of drinks, I was ready to scoot the brothers out the door and see everything up close. On one of her trips to the bathroom, I followed her and pushed her into a dark corner.

"What are you doing?" She smiled and pushed me away, teasing.

"I'm going to kiss my wife," I replied, hoping I didn't get a sarcastic response for once. Instead, she simply leaned in and kissed me. As much as I wanted to rip her clothes off and take her right there in that corner with everyone in the next room—I knew better. I knew we had all the time in the world to consummate our vows, to make love, to do it all, yet we had very few nights in a penthouse above a beautiful city to share with friends old or new.

"I asked Sean and Pearse to take Toby out on the town," she told me. "They promised they would leave here by one." She looked to the clock on the wall. "That gives us half an hour to be polite, then I'm gonna see if you remembered your panties or not." She tugged at my dress and I shooed her away.

"Toby's been here a million times, he should be the one showing them around town," I said as we walked back to the seating area. "Has he ever been to the Fruit and Nut Bar?" I laughed.

"I doubt it. He embarrasses easily. Of course he's drunk enough tonight that he might enjoy himself." She laughed.

"Where's Toby staying?"

"All three guys are staying at the apartment tonight. Sean already checked them out of their hotel. I figured since we have the penthouse here for two nights, they could save some hotel money. I didn't know Toby was coming until after I already made the promise to Sean."

"We have the penthouse until Thursday? Cool." I was excited about taking advantage of the Jacuzzi tub in the mornings.

"Consider this the honeymoon suite. Oh, our flight leaves Thursday at one and Toby is going back with us. The Pollard brothers leave in the morning, so you'll have to say good-bye tonight."

It hadn't occurred to me that I would have to bid farewell to our friends so soon. I was growing rather attached to the pair. I almost cried at the thought. "Can we keep them, please?"

"We'll see them in a few months at home. Nora would kill us if we didn't send Sean home. He has pipes to fix." She started to tell the story.

"I heard. Sounds like you got an earful of Irish lass lashing," I said to Sam, then sat back on the sofa and rested my head on Pearse's shoulder. "You're leaving us tomorrow. Whatever will I do without my male counterpart?"

"Ah, you'll survive." He looked a little disheartened. He started to speak again but was interrupted by Toby.

"I'd like to make one more toast on this grand, sloppy drunk, beautiful occasion." Toby rocked as he spoke. "To love. May it burn brightest in the darkest hours and never flicker in the winds of— I can't remember the rest, but it was nice." He held up his empty glass and we all stood to join him.

We started to sit when Sean stepped in. "We should leave these beautiful ladies to do what they may. I'd like to make a toast as well before we depart." He raised his glass. "May joy and peace surround you, contentment latch your door; and happiness be with you now, and bless you ever more. Slainte."

"Slainte," we all repeated to the best of our ability.

I looked to Pearse who said nothing. He just set down his

glass and walked toward the elevator. "Have you no parting words? We won't see you again for a few months, so I at least get a hug from the maid of honor?"

Pearse held his head down and shrugged. Sean rushed to his defense. "He's an emotional little bugger. Never has been good with good-byes." Then Sean gave me a huge hug and followed up with one for Sam. "We'll take good care of your drunken American brother," he assured Sam.

"Take him to the Fruit and Nut Bar," Sam whispered loud enough for the sober folks to hear. Toby was busy hugging the caterers. "He blushes easily," she said as she handed him a wad of cash and winked.

"It will be my pleasure, lass. Thank you for a wonderful experience. I am proud to know you." Sean grabbed Toby by the shoulders and led him to the elevator.

"See you tomorrow, sisters." Toby waved.

Finally Pearse spoke. "Not to be the trite Irishman, but I do have a farewell toast." He forced a smile. "May the road rise up to meet you. May the wind be always at your backs. May the sun shine warm upon your faces; may the rains fall soft upon your fields and until we meet again, may God hold you in the palm of His hand."

"Thank you Pearse. That was lovely." Sam gave him a hug and kiss. "This isn't good-bye, just farewell until a later day."

He returned the affection. "Take care of my girl." It seemed like it was all he could say.

"I'll see you soon and we'll continue our conversation from the shower." I'd tried to make him laugh, but failed. "I'll call you on Friday."

"I love you," he replied and stepped on the elevator.

I called after him as the elevator doors closed. "I love you too Pearson Pollard!"

I never did get a hug.

The friendly waiters were paid and on their way down the elevator and Sam and I were alone at last. I was exhausted but never would have admitted to it. I could tell by Sam's laugh that she had gotten her second wind and was ready to start our own party. "I'd like to make a toast." She held up her glass.

I poured myself a drink and stood across from her, trying not to roll my eyes. "Okay, go ahead."

"I was just kidding," she snickered. "So, do the Irish have a toast for every occasion?"

"Oh, thank God. One more trite toast and I was gonna jump off the roof. Maybe it's a man thing, even Toby added to the clichés this evening."

"I'd be surprised if he lasted another hour tonight. He went straight from working fourteen hours at night, getting everything signed off so he could leave, then hopping onto the four-hour train ride from Paris that got him here at seven. I didn't think he would make it. I called him last night to ask how Amelia was doing, and I told him our plans because I was about to burst."

"So he's done with the Paris renovation?" Usually Toby was gone for months at a time; I was surprised he could abandon the job so quickly.

"Not really. We talked for a while about families, wives, children and I think it occurred to him that he needed to prioritize before it was too late." She took a deep breath. "I told him I would go back to France and finish things up if he needed me to."

I tried not to blow up. "So what are your priorities?" Obviously planning our reception and getting back to our life wasn't one of them.

"Funny, that's what he said. We decided to send Mom. She would love a break from Dad." Sam plopped herself down onto the sofa. "Come join me, Missus Laine."

"Missus Laine?"

"Well, shouldn't one of us change our last name? I guess I could be Missus O'Connor." She repeated it a few more times. "You know, Dani Laine sounds better than Sam O'Connor."

I repeated the names. "Dani Laine sounds like a stripper's name. Sam O'Connor sounds like a news reporter."

"New career paths for both of us," she teased.

"Well, what I meant before was that I wouldn't be Missus Laine, I would be Doctor Laine, if you wanna get technical."

"My parents would love that. They always wanted a doctor in the family." She rested her head on my shoulder.

"Still, I think for the sake of your hotel business, and my being so attached to my own name, we ought to just keep the names as they read on our passports," I suggested.

"You're just too cheap to get a new passport, aren't you?"

"You know me so well." She really did. "Plus I finally got a good photo, I wouldn't want to reshoot."

"Okay, Doctor O'Connor, you keep your name. I'll continue to be named after a hotel chain. It's fine." She faked a sniffle.

"You are more than welcome to be Missus O'Connor."

"I appreciate that, Doc. But it took me months to get maintenance to paint my name on my office door. I wouldn't want to go through all that paperwork again."

"Whatever. You just know with that girly face and those delicate features that you are more a Laine than an O'Connor." I stroked her soft skin.

"Well, I do have all those new business cards." She made another excuse. "Plus O'Connor is a bit brazen."

"Yes, she is." I unzipped her dress to prove just how brazen we O'Connors really were.

It wasn't like it was the first time we had sex, but it was the first intimacy we shared as a married couple. I admit that I was as nervous as a teenage virgin on her wedding night. Perhaps part of me expected something to be different about it. Maybe I expected more passion, or worse, perhaps I feared the passion would be gone since we entered the institution of marriage.

I paced the room while waiting for Sam to get out of the bathtub. I thought about joining her, but didn't want figure out the hooks on my lingerie again if I had to get redressed. So, I waited impatiently and continued to pace. Every few minutes, I sat on the edge of the bed and tried to look seductive. It wasn't easy for me to look seductive when I was uncomfortable in my red bustier and black thong. After about half an hour, I started to feel stupid and decided I should change into the simple black lace teddy I had hidden in my luggage. I tiptoed to the bathroom door and peeked through the keyhole. I didn't see Sam, but I heard the tub draining, so I figured I had a few more minutes.

I struggled with the hooks on the bustier and gave up on the last three. I decided it would be easier to pull the thing over my head like a T-shirt rather than opening it like a vest. It never occurred to me that it was too form-fitting to simply pull off, so I tried to push it down over my hips instead. That didn't work either, so I sat on the bed and struggled with the remaining hooks and realized that they were bent from the turmoil. I started to sweat a little and told myself to stay calm. The bustier was stuck around my hips with the breast part resting inches below my breasts. I tried pushing the center back and forth hoping the hooks would miraculously follow suit with the others. No luck. I thought maybe I could use my teeth to bend the hooks, so I curled up on the floor in the fetal position and tried to get my head low enough to reach the bottom of the garment. That's when Sam exited the bathroom—so much for looking seductive.

"Oh, Dani. Starting without me?" Sam stood in the doorway. The bathroom light shone behind her and I could see the silhouette of her body though the thin silk of her mid-length, white babydoll nightie.

I swallowed hard and forgot my predicament while I admired her beauty. "You look amazing, Sam."

"You look—" She tilted her head and smiled. "You look uncomfortable."

I glanced down at the red bustier and laughed. "I decided I wanted to put on a teddy. I wasn't prepared for the difficult architecture of trashy lingerie." I pulled myself up on the bed. "The hooks are jammed."

I could smell the sweet scent of her powder as she glided toward me. "Perhaps you should have used duct tape like you did on your dress." She leaned over me and fought with the first hook. "It's really stuck."

"I know!" I wanted to cry, but laughed instead. "I'm such a freak."

"I bet you looked beautiful before disaster struck." She continued to fight with the hooks and finally freed two of the three.

I lay there on the bed feeling tremendously embarrassed and aroused by the way she was forcing me out of my clothes.

"Count on me to ruin our wedding night." I smiled and watched her eyes as she focused on the last hook.

"You didn't ruin anything, Doc. I'm gonna have to break this last one. It might hurt a little." She placed both her hands inside the bustier and yanked the fabric with all her might.

I heard the ripping of the lace and felt it scratch my skin as it separated.

"There," she said, "I think you're a free woman. Did that hurt?"

"It'll only hurt if I'm ever free of you." It seemed like a corny thing to say, but the way she was looking at me made me think of all the times ahead—catastrophes and all.

"That, my love, will never happen." She lay next to me and rested her head on my shoulder.

I closed my eyes and inhaled her scent. I breathed in the moment and made a mental note to remember that exact moment for the rest of my life. I was sure that over the years I would tell many people the funny tale of how I got stuck in lingerie, but I knew I could never convey the love I felt for the woman who saved me from it.

She whispered something in my ear and it didn't register. I didn't want to ask her to repeat it, so I just smiled and nodded. I guess she said something about wanting me, because a second later she kissed my shoulder and moved her way over to my neck. She focused her attention all around my neck and below each ear before gently pressing her lips against my own. We kissed slowly and sweetly at first before the want kicked in and the kisses became desperate and breathtaking.

As she climbed on top of me, I wrapped my arms around her body and enjoyed the feeling of silk against my breasts. We continued the frantic kisses for what seemed like hours, then she placed her hand behind my neck, supporting my head and placed the other hand tenderly against my cheek.

"I want to make love to my wife," she whispered. "My beautiful, funny, sexy wife." She looked deep into my eyes and I felt truly loved.

I wasn't sure how to respond, or even if I should say anything at all. I was usually pretty sarcastic when it came to talking during sex, but it didn't seem that humor would be welcomed at that exact occasion. My mind kind of froze up and I must have stared at her a little too long.

"Are you okay, Dani?" She caressed my cheek and stroked my hair.

"I love you, Sam." I kissed her neck and slid my hands across the cool silk to her breasts.

A soft moan rolled from her throat and I felt that I said and did the right thing. I elected not to speak again, rather to show my new wife how much I really did love her.

I slept for about an hour after our private celebration and was wide awake before the sun came up. Sam was lying next to me, snoring away. Her naked body was warm against mine, and I knew there was no way I would go back to sleep, so I just lay there listening to her. It's amazing, the feeling you get, when you love someone so much. I got a knot in my stomach just from her mere presence. I wanted to touch her, to stroke her hair, to listen to her heartbeat and feel her warmth. Sam was the first person in my life who ever made me truly understand affection.

Kissing wasn't strictly for the sake of kissing with Sam. Kissing her was like taking a breath with her, like, well, it's kind of hard to describe. Sometimes when people fly, they are so terrified that they actually kiss the ground when they land at the airport. I guess it's their way of saying they are thrilled to be home, to have arrived safely. Kissing the ground reassures them that everything is okay. That's kind of what it was like for me to kiss Sam. The kiss was a reminder to my body that I was home where I should be, that I was safe and that everything was okay. We kiss babies on the forehead because they're just so precious that we have to let them know they're loved. At the same time, we take in part of their sweet baby smell and feel the softness of their skin. Kissing Sam was my opportunity to take her in, yet also remind her how precious she was to me. I always tried, with every kiss, to make it so good that she could feel she was loved.

With other people, a quick peck on the lips would suffice. For me, when it came to my Sam, I needed more than a peck. Even when she was scurrying out the door, I made a point to close my eyes and touch her face. She always did the same in return.

As the sun started to rise, I could see more and more of Sam's outline next to me. I wanted to just wrap myself around her, like a human blanket that would always keep her warm. I loved waking up next to her—it was continually the best part of my day. Even when we had things to do and places to be, we made a point to take the few extra minutes every morning to just be us. We were the us, alone together for that last five minutes before the world would start revolving around other things. We would hold each other a little tighter, crawl up against one another, and bury our faces on each other's neck. We would take in the sounds and smells of the other—her sweet, fading perfume and her quiet morning breathing. Her breathing wasn't so quiet that particular morning, but on most occasions she was very sweet.

I rolled onto my side and backed my body into hers. She usually took the hint, even when she was sleeping. Today was no different as she wrapped her arm around me, pulled me closer and buried her face into my back. I could tell she was still asleep, but her snoring ceased. My heart started beating faster and my own breathing grew heavier. It wasn't that I was aroused and wanted sex. It was that the feeling I got when I was that close to her just made me want to crawl inside her soul, think her thoughts and see the world through her eyes.

Beyond teaching me about affection, Sam also taught me about sex and love. The drunken nights in college with nameless strangers were for the sole purpose of sex itself. Intimacy with the various men and women of my past was for affection or the simplistic orgasm. Being physical with Sam was different. It wasn't about the pleasure that I could feel myself, or about my human need to be touched. It was about my need to touch her, to feel that closeness, to bring her pleasure. I had never been comfortable with the term making love as a euphemism for sex. I always hated it when people would remark about casual sex by saying "We made love after we left the bar." To be blunt, it would have been better to refer to the drunken encounters as simply fucking. If you're going to get drunk and exploit a stranger for your own pleasure, then why not be just as vulgar in how you refer to it? Why not just say, "I got drunk, picked up a chick and fucked her?" Why not save the expression making love for when that was the reality of it? I would imagine there was only a small majority of people in the world who actually got to experience the true feeling of loving someone so much that being intimate with them could be defined as making love. To love someone so much that you want to kiss, and touch, and feel every inch of them, is such a gift. That was the gift that Sam gave me. That feeling of her closeness was the greatest gift that had ever been bestowed upon me. I prayed she felt the same, and the way she held me so tightly that morning told me that she did.

The sun was fully up and the sounds from the city grew louder with every passing moment. I wasn't sure if I had drifted back to sleep or if I had lain there resting in my own thoughts. I felt Sam stretch and let out a little moan which told me she was awake. "Morning, baby. How'd you sleep?"

She kissed my neck and didn't respond.

"What do you want to do on our one and only honeymoon day?" I was hoping she had it all planned out.

She rubbed her hand up and down my side and didn't say anything.

The fact that she wasn't speaking freaked me out a little. I thought maybe I was in some sort of weird dream where I woke up with my back to my new wife and when I rolled over to face her I would find some sort of three-eyed beast. I decided to give it one last try before I faced the nightmare. "You were snoring." If that didn't get her, nothing would.

"I don't snore," she whispered and I knew I was safely in the arms of my two-eyed wife.

"I learned something about you this morning. In retrospect, I've known it all along, but it came to fruition today."

"Oh, do tell." She sounded like she expected something silly.

"You don't snore when you hold me. You can lie next to me for hours and sound like a chainsaw, but the minute you wrap your arms around me, the snoring disappears." I was smiling just from remembering the feeling.

"Maybe you found a way to quiet the three-eyed beast." Her reference to my nightmare scenario startled me and I realized I really was dreaming.

"Dani, wake up. It's almost nine." I felt Sam's breath on my neck.

"I was dreaming that you were snoring." I rolled over to face her.

"I don't snore."

I decided to repeat the statement from my dream to see if I got the same response. If I did I was going to look around for Rod Serling. "I learned something about you this morning. In retrospect, I've known it all along, but it came to fruition today."

"You've already been up? You should have woken me. What came to fruition today?"

"You don't snore when you hold me. You can lie next to me for hours and sound like a chainsaw, but the minute you wrap your arms around me, the snoring disappears." The déjà vu was grueling.

"Then I guess I sleep more peacefully knowing you're next to me. I don't have to be loud to scare off my nightmares."

I found it interesting that she mentioned nightmares. I wondered if she had them as often as I did. "That may be it."

"Either that or else when I raise my arm up, my body shifts, thus opening my throat and nasal passages eventually allowing the carbon dioxide to exit my body more quietly."

"Yeah. Let's go with the first explanation. I'd rather imagine us sleeping peacefully and not inhaling each other's carbon dioxide." I'd never thought of it that way before. "Wait a minute. Don't we inhale carbon dioxide and exhale carbon monoxide?"

"First of all, Dani, it's too early in our marriage for scientific debate of how things work. We're supposed to be naked and giggling. We can debate nature when we're old and boring. Secondly, you might be a great English teacher, but you would have done awful as a science teacher. Our bodies exhale carbon dioxide. Please tell me you know what we inhale." I could tell she was trying not to laugh at me.

I had to think for a minute. "I'm pretty sure we inhale dioxide and exhale monoxide."

"Oh my God! I can't believe we're even having this conversation. Okay, Doctor Smarty-Pants, when people sit in running cars while the garage doors are closed, what are they doing?"

"Wasting gas?" I knew I was about to be teased for my stupidity.

"Right. They are attempting suicide. The gas that the car emits is carbon monoxide and it's poisonous. If humans emitted carbon monoxide, then we could kill each other in our sleep just by sleeping too closely to someone's breath."

"There have been times when your breath could kill me in my sleep." I chuckled.

"I'm so gonna kick your ass." She climbed on top of me and pinned me down by my arms. "Take that back or I'll break your collarbone."

I took a deep breath. "You know, I may be emitting carbon dioxide, but I'm pretty sure I just inhaled morning breath-oxide."

"You're hysterical." She climbed off me and let me sit up. "Please, for the sake of my sanity, tell me you do know what it is that humans inhale."

"Pollutants? Cocaine? Glue?" I was stalling.

"Doc, you're killing me." She climbed out of bed and walked toward the kitchenette. "You have five minutes to answer or I'm revoking your doctor title."

Of course I remembered learning about how our body takes in oxygen, mixes it with carbon and releases carbon dioxide. Perhaps I had a lapse in memory that morning. Once I remembered the word I was looking for was oxygen the subject had been dropped. It was strange that I couldn't remember such an obvious thing, and I chalked it up to being tired.

"What's for breakfast?" I was sure she made arrangements for something.

Just like at home, her reply was the same. "Breakfast is in the microwave."

I opened the door to the little microwave and inside was a box of Krispy Kreme donuts, just like she had done on my birthday. "Hey, big spender. Did you buy these yourself? Or did Mr. Kreme himself come make them fresh in our kitchen?"

"You'd be surprised. I had those flown in from the closest store in Liverpool."

"So we're having breakfast from England this morning. We're such the jet-setters. What's for lunch? A Happy Meal from Japan?"

"You're awfully feisty today." She took a donut. "What's gotten into you?"

"Oxygen."

Chapter 13

We decided we should do a little sight seeing before we flew back to the States. I wanted to take a train and view the countryside, but we really didn't have time for that. We decided we would take a tour of the Anne Frank Huis and maybe spend a little time buying tacky souvenirs from the Red Light District. We stopped by the apartment to invite Toby to join us. He insisted that we spend the day alone like most people do on their honeymoon. His appearance indicated that he was too hung over to function anyway, so we didn't persist. We asked him if he went to the Fruit and Nut Bar and he shut the door in our faces. We took that as a yes.

We didn't have to wait in line long for the tour of the house. I was surprised that we were actually allowed to walk through the upstairs. The downstairs had been transformed into a museum, but the upstairs had been left as it was during the Frank family's hiding. Glass had been placed over parts of the walls where Anne had hung pictures, magazine clippings and other things a young girl would admire. Some of the rooms were bigger than I expected, but then again if I had to stay inside those walls for that long of time, I'm sure the space would seem much smaller.

It was hard to get a good look at everything because of all the tourists and I did begin to feel a little claustrophobic and nauseated. I could only imagine what it must have been like for the family. I realized how hard it must have been to know that the world was still functioning below your windows, and you couldn't witness any of it. To be a child and not get to play in the streets; to hear the beautiful bells coming from the majestic buildings, yet never having the freedom to visit the insides of the buildings. I wondered what people who survived that experience thought of the modern day Amsterdam. Was it ironic to know that at one time some people didn't have the freedom to simply walk the streets, whereas nowadays everyone visited Amsterdam because it's a place where you can do damned near anything. I wondered what it would be like to be locked in a building above the canals sixty years later and try to imagine what was happening below—to know that you were within walking distance to something like the Red Light District, yet the only thing you could see from your window was a tree.

Perhaps it seems like a depressing tour to take on the day after your wedding. I guess it depends on how you look at it. Although it's a reminder of the atrocities of the past, the story behind it does show that there is kindness in humanity. It does make you think about the good and bad in people, and it reminds you to love kindly and appreciate what you have in your own little space of the world.

Sam and I didn't talk much about the experience other than the obvious observations. It's kind of personal for everyone, I guess—the feelings that rush through you when you face a part of history. Some things affect people differently. I was one who was on the verge of tears the whole time, where Sam appeared to be flatout terrified by all of it.

It took a while to snap back to the modern day world after the tour. We had lunch at a little café off the square and walked through some shops. We debated the idea of hitting the antique stores, but I had confronted enough history for one day. I had heard about an artist whose studio was nearby, so I talked Sam into walking over to see her work. Sam was a bit of an art elitist, so I was hoping the rumors of the artist's talent were true. I could also tell that the morning's event was weighing heavy on her mind and I hoped art would be a nice distraction.

As we rounded the street corner near her studio, we were met with a bunch of cats. There must have been at least twenty of them just lounging around the sidewalk—playing, bathing, eating and fighting.

"What's the term for a group of cats? A gaggle?" I asked, hoping to lighten the mood.

"No, a gaggle is for geese. I think it's a brood."

"A brood of cats." It didn't sound right to me. "No. Maybe it's a murder?"

"A murder is for crows and NFL players with good attorneys." She laughed. "Maybe it's army, or colony. Maybe it's a band?"

"Armies and colonies are for ants. And there's no way it could be a band," I submitted.

"Why can't it be a band?"

"Because they don't have any instruments." I knew she would set me up. "I think it's a litter."

"Litters are for puppies and kittens, Doc. Maybe it's a flock of cats or a mustering."

"No. How about a rhumba? That sounds familiar." I opened the door to the studio and let Sam walk in before me.

She thought for a moment. "No, a rhumba is a group of rattlesnakes."

"How on earth would you know that?" I was impressed.

"Hello," she sang. "Yet another thing I learned in science class."

"You learned what a group of rattlesnakes is called, but you can't remember what a group of cats is?" I teased.

A voice came from behind me. "It's a clowder. Or some people say clutter." Sam and I just stared at the woman who filled up the room with wild hair and oversized tie-dyed overalls. "A group of cats is called a clowder or a clutter. Personally, I call them a pain in my ass, but I feed them anyway."

I realized she was the artist. The paint on her hands kind of gave it away. "You must get that question a lot?"

"Almost once a week in every language imaginable. I finally looked it up on the Internet so I could have an educated response." She wiped her hands on her capri pants and introduced herself. "I'm Magda Kent. Welcome to my world of color. Make yourselves at home, feel free to take a cat on your way out."

"Thank you." We had been so wrapped up in our animal conversation that I didn't even notice the walls around us. Her work was very bold and definitely what I would consider abstract. Each piece was at least four feet tall and became more interesting the farther away you stood from it. Most of the art Sam and I collected told a story through the minute details. Magda's work could only be viewed from across the room. Sam and I went off in different directions to stay out of the other's line of sight. I was particularly affected by one of the darker images. I kept taking steps backward and saw more and more of what she was trying to convey.

"It's very dark," Magda whispered while slowly approaching. "What do you see?"

I was afraid I would insult her if I didn't see the exact image she had intended. "I see lots of things."

"What two images strike you the most? It's okay, you won't hurt my feelings if you say it's all just a big blur." Her accent was indeterminable.

"I see a tree in the far background?" I sounded like the Dutch bicycle girl, neither making a statement nor asking a question.

"That could very well be a tree." She smiled. "What else?"

"I'm getting a sense of fear or angst. Maybe anger?"

"What's causing that emotion?" She put her arm across my shoulders.

"I don't know really. There seems to be a face. It's pale, like innocence, maybe?" I felt as though I was being tested on some material I had never read.

"A face within the tree." She sighed. "I believe you and I have similar eyes, my American friend. What story do you know of innocence, fear and the image of a tree?"

The answer was obvious given the neighborhood. "Anne Frank."

"It's titled Chestnut," she whispered and walked away.

I looked at a few more pieces, spending enough time with them to find the story. Once I thought I knew what I was looking at, I read the title to see if I really did have a vision similar to Magda's. I was accurate for the most part. I found Sam on the second floor of the studio sitting in a chair staring at an unfinished canvas. "Taking a break?" I asked and kissed the top of her head.

"No. I really like this one. I think I'm stumped though.

What do you see?"

"You know art perception is different for everyone. I may see a walrus and you may see a rhumba of rattlers," I joked.

"I see fireworks. I see a fading white firework in a midnight sky. The red around it seems like smoke from an earlier burst." She tilted her head sideways. "It reminds me of you and what I said yesterday about how you cry at the vibrancy of the colors."

I sat down next to her. "I see a shoe."

"You got to be kidding me. What kind of shoe? There's no laces."

"You know, like the souvenir shoes they sell here. A wooden shoe." I took her hand and pointed to the painting. "See, that's the tip." I moved her fingers downward and to the right. "That's the sole, and the heel." I felt Magda's presence behind us, but didn't want to break Sam's focus on the painting to ask.

"A wooden shoe. Hmmm. I still see a firework and how it must look fading through your eyes." She sniffed.

"You know, those were beautiful vows. I meant to tell you that. I believe there is a poet in you somewhere. I couldn't have asked for better words to be spoken on our wedding day." I wiped the tear off her cheek and kissed the hand that was still in mine.

"I loved what you said too. You're the true poet of our family." She squeezed my hand.

I remembered that Magda was standing behind us and I didn't want her to feel awkward so I changed the subject. "Did you see all the others downstairs? I don't think these pieces up here are for the public to view yet."

"I did. I was just drawn upstairs. I should have asked." She stood without taking her eyes off the painting.

"It's fine," Magda said. "I told you to make yourselves at home." She walked toward us. "Please sit back down and enjoy looking. Can I offer you anything? A beer, wine, cookie, drugs?"

I couldn't help but laugh. I couldn't imagine a gallery in Dallas offering drugs. "I would love a beer, Magda. Thank you."

Sam smiled and finally looked away from the painting. "I'd

appreciate a beer and whatever else you're offering."

Magda stood and called down the stairs. "Ursula!"

"What Mags?" an annoyed voice screamed back.

"Bring up three beers and a left-handed cigarette." Magda winked. But Ursula didn't respond. "Ursula!"

"I heard you already!" The words were followed by a series of profanities.

"Are you from Amsterdam, Magda?" Sam asked.

"I am from New Zealand. I moved here about twenty years ago. I also have a house in Manhattan."

Sam asked, "Art has been good to you?" I was surprised she would inquire about someone's finances.

Magda didn't seem to care. "The stock market was good to me. Intel, Google, oil. Art is just what completes me. Watercolor, acrylics, oil."

"Completes you?" I often felt that way about my writing, but had never heard anyone else put it so profoundly.

"You might call it anxiety or compulsiveness. I get a thought in my head and I can't sit still until I find a way to convey it. Sometimes I can't sleep for days until my thoughts take shape on the canvas."

A young, plump blonde came up the stairs with a tray of beer. "Here's your beer your royal ass holiness." Ursula shoved the beer into Magda's open arms.

"Thank you dear. Ladies, this is my daughter, Ursula."

"I'm Sam, this is Dani." She extended her hand.

"Whatever." She didn't return the handshake.

"If I eavesdropped correctly, Ursula, these ladies came to Amsterdam to get married." She glanced at us, and we nodded to confirm.

"Really? Well, if that's true, you really oughta like the shoe piece." She pointed at the unfinished painting and snickered.

Magda chuckled in return. "I'll explain it to them."

"If you're gonna get stoned with the Americans, I'm gonna go over to Freddie's house. I'll finish the brushes tomorrow, Mom."

"That's fine. Put up the closed sign and lock the door on your way out."

"Whatever." Ursula marched back down the stairs in a huff.

"Kids," Magda sighed and rolled her eyes. "She wants to go back to New York. I keep telling her that people would kill to live over here. She doesn't care. She dropped out of college and is apparently in search of herself. I told her she needed to find herself soon or she would find herself living outside with the cats."

"Oh, to be young again." I flashed back to my own teenage years.

Sam stared at the painting again. "What did she mean about the shoe piece?"

"Let's smoke some of this first. It will be much more amusing if you're stoned." Magda lit the joint and took a long drag. "Of course, everything's more amusing when you're stoned." She passed it to Sam who followed suit.

"Is the price more amusing when you're high?" I asked, taking the J from Sam.

"There is nothing funny about money," Sam and Magda both said, almost in unison. I knew immediately they had to be distant relatives.

"You want to buy this one, eh? I figured you would when I saw how Sam here reacted." Magda opened a Heineken with her belt buckle.

I took another hit off the joint and laughed at the sight of a gray-haired woman smacking a bottle on her midsection. "I'm sorry, I didn't mean to laugh. Yes, I'd like to buy this piece for my wife." I started laughing again when I said the word wife. I guess it still seemed foreign to me.

"Aren't you a cheap stoner?" Sam laughed. "Two hits and you're in hysterics." She was bent over laughing. "Oh, shit. So am I."

Magda opened the other two bottles and sat back down. "I pack a good spleef."

The word spleef made me snort. "Oh, hell. I'm sorry Magda. What's in this stuff?"

"Only the best for my best customers." She laughed along with us. "This piece isn't finished."

Sam was suddenly sober. "It's perfect the way it is. Please don't change a thing. We'll pay extra if you stop now." She almost sounded panicked.

"Eight thousand Euro," Magda burst out.

I stared at her, waiting to see if she was serious.

"Six thousand?" She sipped her beer.

I continued to stare and tried to keep a straight face.

"Four thousand and I'll throw in a joint for the road." Magda stared back at me, completely serious.

"You got a deal. But don't change a thing." I clinked my Heineken against hers.

Sam finally smiled again. "What do you call this piece anyway?"

Magda fell into a fit of hysterics. She tried to say it four times before we could finally understand her. "I call it Wooden Shoe Marry Me."

The three of us laughed so hard that we cried.

We left the Magda Kent studio in great spirits. Arrangements were made to have the painting shipped, but we did get the joint the second my credit card was approved. We were able to escape without taking any of the cats away from the clutter. We also made a promise to visit Magda and Ursula the next time we were in New York the same time they were. I couldn't tell if Magda really liked us or was just after our money. If she got all her potential buyers stoned, she probably made a killing. The afternoon with the artist did make for a great memory, and the painting was the perfect wedding gift, even if that wasn't the real title of the piece. For all we knew, she and Ursula pulled that heist on every newlywed couple. Regardless, it was a beautiful painting and a great ending to our two-week vacation.

We had a nice dinner with Toby who had made little recovery from the excessive night before, and headed back to the hotel relatively early so we had time to relax before facing the real world of airports and Dallas traffic. Part of me was anxious to get home to see my brother and Amelia, but the other part of me wanted to stay in Amsterdam where I could have Sam all to myself. We had fifteen hours until we had to leave for the airport, and we planned on making the most of it by cramming an entire honeymoon into one night. I figured there were three essential parts to any honeymoon: romance, laughter and sex. Perhaps those were the three characteristics of a relationship, and if one disappeared, the other two were sure to follow. Sam and I never had a problem in the laughter category. She made me laugh more than anyone I had ever met—probably because she let me be myself, and deep down inside I was nothing but a huge goofball. We were pretty regular in the sex category as well. Sure, there were weeks, even months that passed without sex, but when we made the effort, it was always passionate and fulfilling. Romance wasn't one of our strong suits. Being a bumbling idiot when it came to quiet intimacy made it hard for me to attempt romance without laughter. Sam was a bit of a gorilla when it came to the gentleness of love. Romance between us could best be defined by the image of a donkey courting a walrus.

I thought it would be nice on our last night to dip our feet into the pool of romance, so to speak. While Sam finished her packing, I filled the Jacuzzi tub with bubbles and rose petals and lit candles in the bathroom and bedroom of the penthouse. Sam managed to set her favorite sweater on fire when she blindly tossed it over her shoulder thinking it would land on the chair behind her. Instead it landed on a vase filled with four floating votive candles. Rather than pushing the sweater into the water-filled vase, she grabbed the burning cardigan and rushed it to the bathroom just as I was climbing into the tub. Her first instinct was to toss the sweater into the sink and turn on the faucet, but when she saw that the tub was already full, she quickly tossed the sweater in and stood beside me screaming—not noticing all the rose petals or the fact that I was naked.

"Sam, why did you just throw a flaming cloth into our bubble bath?" The whole incident seemed impossible.

"I didn't know you lit torches all over the room. I was setting my sweater aside to wear on the plane tomorrow and it went up in flames." She was breathing heavily.

"Ah." I stared as the charred remains floated to the top of the water. "But why did you decide to put the blazing garment in the tub?"

"Look, Doc, I'm not sure how fast wool burns. I had to act fast or this whole place could have gone aflame." She was trying not to laugh.

"How long does it take to cook lamb chops?" I asked.

"I don't know, why?"

"That might give us an idea about how long it takes for wool to burn." I pulled on a robe. "Once again the giant oaf has ruined the romance of the evening. Thanks a lot."

"Don't be so dramatic. We can drain the tub and draw a new bath. There's plenty of romance to be had here." She skimmed some rose petals off the surface of the water.

"It kind of smells like burning hair in here." I took a deep breath. "And a little like gas."

"Shut up." She blushed. "You know I get fear farts."

"What the hell are fear farts?" I almost couldn't ask.

She sat on the edge of the tub and held her head down. For a moment I thought she was crying, then I realized she was in heavy giggle mode—snorts and all. "I thought I was going to burn down the hotel, Doc. I freaked out a little, and my body reacted. Some people release adrenaline. I release gas."

I sat next to her on the edge of the tub and snorted along with her. "Baby, you are full of surprises."

She blushed. "I'm full of something."

"You are indeed." I rested my head on her shoulder. "And that's why I love you, fear farts and all."

"Can we skip the romance and just go straight to the bedroom?" She kissed my forehead.

"Samantha Laine," I sighed.

"Yes, Doc?"

"There is nothing in this world that I would like less." I burst out laughing and ran from the bathroom.

She chased after me and tackled me on the ash-covered bedroom floor. "Wanna go to a bar?"

"Meet me at the elevator in ten minutes." I pushed her off me and went to get dressed.

Many bars in Amsterdam sported a rainbow flag out front. That didn't necessarily mean they were exclusively gay bars, just that they welcomed folks like us. We decided it best to stay close to the hotel, so we walked two doors down to a bar that flew the flag and also advertised live music on Wednesdays. We found a booth in a dark corner and ordered some drinks from a chubby Dutch woman who spoke no English and seemingly had no patience for our attempt at her language. The entire time we were in Holland, we were met with nothing but kindness from friendly people. So the general attitude in that bar threw us for a loop, but we stayed anyway hoping for one final adventure.

According to a sign inside, Wednesday's live band had cancelled due to faulty equipment, so we were stuck with the lovely sound of fifties music from a broken jukebox. The same song would play twice, sometimes three times, in a row. I was reminded of Sean's story about Pearse and the diversity of bars, and their music, drinks and people. This particular bar had no diversity, and I thought maybe we were being tested on Pearse's theory. After our first round of drinks, the waitress brought us a plate of something that appeared to be deep fried balls. We tried to explain to her that we hadn't ordered food. We could only assume that all patrons were expected to eat, because she indicated that we wouldn't be served any more beer until we had at least tasted one of the greasy orbs.

I was reminded of the first time I tried Rocky Mountain oysters. I was eleven years old and thought they were pretty darned good, kind of like chicken fried beef. When my sister told me they were bull's balls, I screamed in horror, puked on my brother's shoes and ran from the restaurant in tears. Over the years I learned to appreciate bull's balls as a strange western delicacy. I felt like my willingness to eat them made me more of a cowgirl. The greasy concoction in the bar that night in Amsterdam did not have the texture of beef or any other animal that I could decipher. They were pretty much just fatty and bland with a hint of spice. The fact that they were sort of runny in the middle wasn't a great selling point either. I forced myself to chew and swallow a small piece of one then waited a minute before moving to make sure the food didn't resurface. Sam did the same and even managed to force a smile. The waitress stood her ground, watching us eat. She kept pointing at the plate and tapping her watch. We took this to mean that time was of the essence—perhaps they would expire if not eaten within a certain time frame. My fear was that they would regain their shape and crawl off the table, so I forced the entire wad into my mouth and chewed as quickly as I could.

"I can't believe you just did that." Sam stared at me in awe.

I continued to chew, unable to swallow.

"Doc, swallow." Sam patted me on the back.

Tears started rolling down my cheeks. "I can't," I said with a full mouth.

"Then spit it out." She handed me a napkin.

"I'm afraid to." I looked at the waitress who was watching me intently. "She might beat me up," I mumbled with a full mouth.

Sam looked back at the burly waitress. "We're in this together." She shoved a ball in her mouth and chewed.

The look on her face was priceless and I almost choked when I saw her eyes start to water. "Good, eh?"

Sam nodded and continued to chew for a good two minutes. We both sat there chewing like we had just eaten deep fried gum. The waitress waited with her arms crossed and smiled. Finally I was able to swallow. I took a deep breath and opened my mouth to prove I had finished my appetizer. I watched Sam for another minute before she finally forced the meat down her own throat. "Bier." She pleaded to the waitress and held her hands in a praying gesture. "Bier!"

The waitress shook her head and said, "Bitterballen."

"Yeah, no shit?" I smiled.

"Let's hope not." Sam opened her eyes widely. "Sure tastes like it though."

The waitress went to the bar and returned with a tray of eight small glasses. She set four glasses in front of each of us and said, "Juttertje, Grolsch, Juttertje, Grolsch."

We took it to mean that we were supposed to drink them in that particular order. We both nodded—signifying that we agreed to her terms. The waitress pointed to the glasses and repeated her previous explanation. It became obvious that once again we wouldn't be left alone until we forced something down our throats.

"Up for it, dreamer?" I asked Sam whose eyes were still watering.

"Like I said, we're in this together." She picked up the first glass of spiced liquor and tossed the liquid down her throat. She looked at me like it was my turn, but the waitress started clapping in a beat that told us that Sam had to drink all four in a row. Amazingly, she did it—drinking the remaining three glasses in less than twenty seconds.

"Well?" I asked, hoping she was going to live.

"I'm pretty sure you eat the raw meat first then send the alcohol down there to cook it." She fanned her mouth. "I'd do it if I were you. You don't want raw meat congealing in your stomach."

I took a deep breath, held up my first glass for the waitress to see and tossed it back. I enjoyed the spicy flavor and would have preferred it without the beer chaser. When all four glasses were empty, I jokingly let my head fall to the table and pretended to be dead.

Neither Sam nor the waitress showed any concern. "Bier?" asked the Dutch woman.

"Dank u." Sam laughed.

Eventually we were left alone to enjoy each other's company. Well, we were given a small glass of a clear liquid that tasted remarkably thick. Aside from that, we were allowed our preferred small glasses of Grolsch in our dark booth in the corner. It occurred to me later that we did have a romantic evening. What was romance anyway if not being together in a corner of the world, sharing new experiences, new flavors, new gag reflexes? Sam said twice that night that we were in this together. I couldn't think of anything more romantic than two people cooking meat in their stomach the night before they board a plane. I learned that night that you can't force romance, just as you can't force love. They are things that you stumble across spontaneously, hand-in-hand with another. I couldn't have asked for a better ending to our time in Holland.

The night together inspired me to write. Before we went to sleep, I wrote yet another poem for Sam on the hotel stationary and placed it in the bottom of my carry-on. I made a mental note to give it to her on our "paper" anniversary.

I'm your given when you wonder
And your shoulder when you're sad
I'm your lover when you're lonely
Your accomplice when you're bad
I'm the one who'll buy you flowers
Paint you paintings, write you poems
I'm the one who'll always listen
And my arms are always home

You're my given when I wonder
And my shoulder when I'm sad
You're my lover when I'm lonely
My accomplice when I'm bad
You're the one who gives me laughter
Fills my heart, sets the tone
You're the one who always listens
And your arms are always home

Chapter 14

Sam and Toby slept during most of the flight back to the States. I was tired, hung over and a little airsick from fried gravy balls, but I was too excited to sleep. I kept thinking about all the things that lay ahead—a new business in our new building, the wedding reception, our life together. I decided to jot down a few notes on what we could do with the building. Obviously it would have to be remodeled, but beyond that the options were limitless. We could open a brewery, a dance club, art gallery, clothing store, loft apartments, or even our own publishing house. I was really leaning toward the idea of loft apartments with a little café and gallery on the first floor, but I decided not to get too far ahead of myself until we saw the place up close and came up with a list of expenses.

Planning the reception would be pretty easy. The hotel staff would likely take care of everything, as they always did. We just needed to get out some invitations and plan the Pollard brothers' itinerary. I was so excited about Sean and Pearse getting to be a part of it all, and I was more excited to have found a friend with whom I instantly connected so easily. Who would have thought I'd fly halfway around the world and meet someone so much like myself...in the Fruit and Nut Bar of all places? I wondered why it was that I had such a hard time making friends in the past. Maybe because we had finally opened ourselves up for new experiences, we were more capable of letting people into our lives. If it wasn't for Pearse and Sean, we wouldn't have gotten married. We would have probably dragged our feet and gone home to further procrastination. I was more grateful to them than I could have ever expressed.

I sat there on the airplane and stared at the seat in front of me while listening to Sam snoring next to me. Something about flying always made me a little philosophical about the world. There we were, thirty-five thousand feet in the air halfway between Europe and the U.S.—basically we were nowhere, yet we had been somewhere and we were going somewhere. At that exact moment, though, we were in limbo. For those of us on the plane, our lives were exactly the same, give or take airsickness and a screaming baby. There was not much any of us could do beyond sleeping, sitting, reading or eating a bag of stale peanuts. We were frozen in time while the world progressed below us. While we listened to our MP3 players and looked forward to a cup of ice and a warm soda, life went on without us. Somewhere below people were buying stocks or stockings. Somewhere there was a man proposing and a woman in tears. Somewhere there was a couple fighting, or making love or both. Somewhere below a person was dying while another was being born. There was a tragedy below, a comedy, a mystery and a great romance. Somewhere there was pain and hunger, and somewhere else there was happiness and greed. Yet we sat on the plane and listened to each other breathe. The immensity of it all made me a little sad.

"Why you crying, Doc?" Sam sat up and placed her hand on mine.

"Just thinking about the world…what lies ahead, and what's left behind." I managed a smile.

"That's awfully deep. I'm just hoping someone picks us up at the airport." She laughed.

I visualized that somewhere in Texas my brother was stuck in traffic on his way to DFW. "I'm sure Jack will be there with bells on," I assured her.

"I hope he wears some pants too. I don't want to relive the scene from last New Year's Eve."

I recalled the scene she was referring to and cringed. "I hope so too, Sam. Hey, thanks for marrying me."

She shot me a funny look. "Thanks for letting me. I'm glad

we got it in before a decade passed. I guess now we just have to spend the rest of our lives looking out for each other, eh?"

"That's right. And making plans…maybe even plan a family." I blushed.

"We could do that. Maybe you could have a baby first, and then I could have one a few years later?" She giggled. "You know, we could go Dutch."

"I was thinking we could go Irish." I smiled remembering Pearse's shower proposal.

"I know you were, and I couldn't imagine a better kid. She'd have two sets of Irish genes with the Irish temper to match, two backgrounds in literature and four green eyes."

"Four green eyes?" I knew what she meant.

"Yes, Doc. A little green-eyed monster." She pointed at my glasses. "Four eyes."

I looked at Toby who was still asleep. "I can't wait to see how his kid turns out."

Sam sighed. "He was a holy terror when we were kids. Let's hope their baby takes after Amelia."

"Especially in the looks department." I pointed out his receding hairline. "I do know for sure, that baby is going to be spoiled and loved."

"Yeah, and on the cover of every gossip magazine in the world," she remarked, referring to the future baby's impending fame from having a famous mother.

"It's amazing that a kid who isn't even born yet is already doomed to tabloid exposure. Poor child will never have a chance at a normal life." I hadn't thought of it before.

"It will seem normal because he or she won't know any differently. That's the price you pay when your mother's a megastar and your father's a dork." Her eyes watered. "I'm so proud of that jackass. Who knew my brother would be capable of settling down to a family."

"Yeah. He got his brain and his heart. The wizard was generous. He's a real man now."

"Great, Doc. Now you're the dork of the family." She pulled herself to her feet. "Switch seats with me. I want to sit next to my brother, and you can look out the window and think your profound little thoughts."

"What makes you think I'm having profound little thoughts?" She knew me well.

"When are you not?" She climbed over me and gave me a kiss before we settled back in.

I sat and watched Sam as she rested her head on her brother's shoulder. Seeing the love between them made me so glad to be a part of the family, even if I was the new dork. As we started our final descent into Dallas, I went back to my profound little thoughts about the world below. Somewhere there was a woman—a pensive lover of the English language. She was sitting at a bar waiting to meet another woman, maybe a funny law student, maybe a beautiful hotel owner. The two of them would meet and fall deeply in love. Maybe they would end up much like us—together for years, married, planning a family and completely happy. Maybe they will teach each other about affection and kindness. Maybe they will approach life with laughter. Maybe they will learn together the wonderfulness of spontaneous romance. Maybe they will get to feel, even if only for a second, the amazing gift of unconditional love between two people. Somewhere out there were couples just like us, maybe they were young and the adventures had just begun. Maybe they were old and gray and their minds held wonderful memories of the life they shared together.

As we walked into baggage claim to be met by Jack, Amelia and a handful of friends, I knew one thing. Out there beyond the sliding glass airport doors was an incredible, bustling world. And the best part of that world was my life with Sam.

Acknowledgements

I'd like to thank the readers who wanted more. Thank you to my mother who taught me that it's okay to dream. Sam, thank you for understanding me and tolerating me anyway; you'll always have my heart. Much gratitude to Linda and all the kind people at Spinsters Ink. A special thank you to Katherine Forrest for her patience, wisdom and kindness.

Publications from Spinsters Ink
P.O. Box 242
Midway, Florida 32343
Phone: 800-301-6860
www.spinstersink.com

ACROSS TIME by Linda Kay Silva. If you believe in soul mates, if you know you've had a past life, then join Jessie in the first of a series of adventures that takes her *Across Time*. ISBN 978-1883523-91-6 $14.95

SELECTIVE MEMORY by Jennifer L. Jordan. A Kristin Ashe Mystery. A classical pianist, who is experiencing profound memory loss after a near-fatal accident, hires private investigator Kristin Ashe to reconstruct her life in the months leading up to the crash. ISBN 978-1-883523-88-6 $14.95

HARD TIMES by Blayne Cooper. Together, Kellie and Lorna navigate through an oppressive, hidden world where lines between right and wrong blur, sexual passion is forbidden but explosive, and love is the biggest risk of all. ISBN 978-1-883523-90-9 $14.95

THE KIND OF GIRL I AM by Julia Watts. Spanning decades, *The Kind of Girl I Am* humorously depicts an extraordinary woman's experiences of triumph, heartbreak, friendship and forbidden love. ISBN 978-1-883523-89-3 $14.95

PIPER'S SOMEDAY by Ruth Perkinson. It seemed as though life couldn't get any worse for feisty, young Piper Leigh Cliff and her three-legged dog, Someday. ISBN 978-1-883523-87-9 $14.95

MERMAID by Michelene Esposito. When May unearths a box in her missing sister's closet she is taken on a journey through her mother's past that leads her not only to Kate but to the choices and compromises, emptiness and fullness, the beauty and jagged pain of love that all women must face.
ISBN 978-1-883523-85-5 $14.95

ASSISTED LIVING by Sheila Ortiz-Taylor. Violet March, an eighty-two-year-old resident of Casa de los Sueños, finally has the opportunity to put years of mystery reading to practical use. One by one her comrades, the Bingos, are dying. Is this natural attrition, or is there a sinister plot afoot?
ISBN 978-1-883523-84-2 $14.95

NIGHT DIVING by Michelene Esposito. Night Diving is both a young woman's coming-out story and a thirty-something coming-of-age journey that proves you can go home again.
ISBN 978-1-883523-52-7 $14.95

FURTHEST FROM THE GATE by Ann Roberts. *Furthest from the Gate* is a humorous chronicle of a woman's coming of age, her complicated relationship with her mother and the responsibilities to family that last a lifetime.
ISBN 978-1-883523-81-7 $14.95

EYES OF GRAY by Dani O'Connor. Grayson Thomas was the typical college senior with typical friends, a typical job and typical insecurities about her future. One Sunday morning, Gray's life became a little less typical, she saw a man clad in black, and started doubting her own sanity.
ISBN 978-1-883523-82-4 $14.95

ORDINARY FURIES by Linda Morgenstein. Tired of hiding, exhausted by her grief after her husband's death, Alexis Pope plunges into the refreshingly frantic world of restaurant resort cooking and dining in the funky chic town of Guerneville, California. ISBN 978-1-883523-83-1 $14.95

A POEM FOR WHAT'S HER NAME by Dani O'Connor. Professor Dani O'Connor had pretty much resigned herself to the fact that there was no such thing as a complete woman. Then out of nowhere, along comes a woman who blows Dani's theory right out of the water.
ISBN 1-883523-78-8 $14.95

WOMEN'S STUDIES by Julia Watts. With humor and heart, *Women's Studies* follows one school year in the lives of three young women and shows that in college, one's extracurricular activities are often much more educational than what goes on in the classroom. ISBN 1-883523-75-3 $14.95

DISORDERLY ATTACHMENTS by Jennifer L. Jordan. The fifth Kristin Ashe Mystery. Kris investigates whether a mansion someone wants to convert into condos is haunted.
ISBN 1-883523-74-5 $14.95

VERA'S STILL POINT by Ruth Perkinson. Vera is reminded of exactly what it is that she has been missing in life.
ISBN 1-883523-73-7 $14.95

OUTRAGEOUS by Sheila Ortiz-Taylor. Arden Benbow, a motorcycle riding, lesbian Latina poet from LA is hired to teach poetry in a small liberal arts college in northwest Florida.
ISBN 1-883523-72-9 $14.95

UNBREAKABLE by Blayne Cooper. The bonds of love and friendship can be as strong as steel. But are they unbreakable?
ISBN 1-883523-76-1 $14.95

ALL BETS OFF by Jaime Clevenger. Bette Lawrence is about to find out how hard life can be for someone of low society standing in the 1900s.
ISBN 1-883523-71-0 $14.95

UNBEARABLE LOSSES by Jennifer L. Jordan. The fourth Kristin Ashe Mystery. Two elderly sisters have hired Kris to discover who is pilfering from their award-winning holiday display. ISBN 1-883523-68-0 $14.95

EXISTING SOLUTIONS by Jennifer L. Jordan. The second Kristin Ashe Mystery. When Kris is hired to find an activist's biological father, things get complicated when she finds herself falling for her client. ISBN 1-883523-69-9 $14.95

A SAFE PLACE TO SLEEP by Jennifer L. Jordan. The first Kristin Ashe Mystery. Kris is approached by well-known lesbian Destiny Greaves with an unusual request. One that will lead Kris to hunt for her own missing childhood pieces.
ISBN 1-883523-70-2 $14.95

Visit
Spinsters Ink
at
SpinstersInk.com
or call our toll-free
number
1-800-301-6860